Star

JOHN SINGLETON

PUFFIN

PUFFIN BOOKS

Published by the Penguin Group
Penguin Books Ltd, 80 Strand, London WC2R 0RL, England
Penguin Group (USA), Inc., 375 Hudson Street, New York, New York 10014, USA
Penguin Books Australia Ltd, 250 Camberwell Road, Camberwell, Victoria 3124, Australia
Penguin Books Canada Ltd, 10 Alcorn Avenue, Toronto, Ontario, Canada M4V 3B2
Penguin Books India (P) Ltd, 11 Community Centre, Panchsheel Park, New Delhi – 110 017, India
Penguin Group (NZ), cnr Airborne and Rosedale Roads, Albany, Auckland 1310, New Zealand
Penguin Books (South Africa) (Pty) Ltd, 24 Sturdee Avenue, Rosebank 2196, South Africa

Penguin Books Ltd, Registered Offices: 80 Strand, London WC2R 0RL, England

www.penguin.com

First published in hardback in Puffin Books 2003
Published in paperback in Puffin Books 2004
1

Set in Adobe Sabon
Typeset by Rowland Phototypesetting Ltd, Bury St Edmunds, Suffolk
Made and printed in England by Clays Ltd, St Ives plc

British Library Cataloguing in Publication Data
A CIP catalogue record for this book is available from the British Library

ISBN 0–141–31611–X

This book is for Paul and Jane,
Andy and Kate, with love

Contents

It was Star saved me from Big Mother. Saved the other kids too. Saved us all. I never said thanks to him. Thanks for getting us out. Never got time in the end.

  Now he's gone – back to where he belongs.

I bet he still keeps an eye on me though.

From the very beginning, Big Mother said I was bad. She said I was bad through and through. But that's a lie. I wasn't. I'd not been bad for ages. She used to say I was from a bad line. But that's a keggin lie. I don't have a line. Not like other kids. Not like the kids in my class. They have dads and grandads and deaddads going back and back. I don't know why she said these things, why she hated me. I had a dad once. Someone said. A woman from Social Services. I looked everywhere, but I couldn't find him. I thought they'd hidden him to punish me. It's all in the Black Book, me having no dad. Big Mother's Black Book. Everything's kept in there. Records, Bad Things. Mostly Bad Things. All the absences, the run-aways, the fights, the bedwets, the medicines, the nurse coming, the doctor, the fosters, the Social Service, the attendance woman, the cuts and bruises, the things lost, stolen, broken, missing.

She knew there was just me. She knows everything. It's in the Book. She knew I was a stray. I think, if you don't belong, you don't count. That's what Big Mother thought.

It was Macker that called them Bad Things. His real name was MacNally, but he was Macker to me. He talked slow and sometimes his nose ran. He wasn't a dimbo and it wasn't his fault. Big Mother didn't like him. She made him wear shorts even in winter, and she used to hit his legs with the Hand so they went red and bluish. Macker cried then and said hitting was a Bad Thing. Macker was different. He said what we didn't want to think about. Everyone else just saw it as normal, the hitting and stuff. But not Macker.

After that, it was Bad Thing this and Bad Thing that. We discovered lots of Bad Things because of Macker. There was Bad Thing porridge. Beatings were number one Bad Things. The Punishment Cupboard was a Big Bad Thing. The Tide-over was a Bad Thing. Wasping was a Bad Thing. And Big Mother was the Biggest Baddest Thing of all.

She only made Macker wear shorts at weekends. She'd smack him Saturdays mainly. Give him Sunday for the red and the blue to fade. That way no evidence. No way the teachers would know about him getting hit. That's why she was the Bad Thing Big Time.

*

When Bad Things happened in The House, she called me into her office and tried to lay it all on me. No, I'd say. You've got a bad record, she'd say. I know you. She could make you cry, could Big Mother. That's the trouble. It's not what's in your line, bad or good, it's what's in your records that counts. Big Mother used to wag the Hand at me and said she knew about me. My sort. But she didn't. She didn't know what goes on inside. No one does. Except maybe Star.

I know Star wanted me to tell all about the Bad Things. So people would know and stop it before it happened again. I asked Miss Chips how could it happen again if we'd got rid of the Bad Things. She's a teacher but she listens to you. She didn't say anything. She put her arm round me and shook her head. I liked her putting an arm round me. Even Star never did that.

But he did get very angry about all the Bad Things.

'We've got to stop them,' he said.

And he did, and this is what I'm telling you about. How he came, what happened then, and how we stopped the Bad Things and, best of all, got rid of Big Mother.

1

Hodge

We call it The House. Everyone else calls it Lazarus House. Lazarus was some dimmo from the Bible who was wrapped up like a mummy and lived in a tomb. He'd like it here, with Big Mummy and all. Yeah, right name in the right place. It smells of mank and bad bodies lot of the time.

My room is at the top, the third floor, and I'm the youngest up here. I'm lying in bed, still awake, listening to the hum of the town and watching the stars. I often lie awake like this. When I was younger, I used to stay awake for hours and stare at the wall. It was where I had the picture of my dad. He was tall with blue eyes and a smile. It was the smile I liked. He was smiling right at me, and I used to smile right back and talk to him. We'd talk about United winning the cup and about going on trips. He wanted to take me to wild places, to where wild animals roam and where he and I could go tracking. He was a bit wild himself, my dad. One day, he came up to The House with a Ferrari, a big red Ferrari, and we went for a spin. That's what he called it: 'a spin'. We did nearly 200 down the motorway. My dad was an expert.

He could do anything then. Mend anything: bike, television, car. I bet he could fix a plane if he wanted.

It wasn't my real dad. It was a made-up one. My real dad had to leave. The social worker said he was tall and handsome and good at football, so I looked through magazines in the school library till I found someone just like that and cut him out. He was wearing sunglasses and looked the business, like a pop star or something. At first, I used to go into town and show people his picture and ask if they'd seen him around. Once someone said he looked like Elvis Presley. Most people thought I was a mental case, but I was young then and didn't realize that sometimes dads just have to go away.

Other times, I used to think he was avoiding me. He didn't want to know me. I must have done something stupid to get him mad like that. So mad he didn't want to see me, talk to me. He probably didn't think I was worth bothering with. I mean, how proud would he be of a son in a stray kids' home? My dad wouldn't have liked that.

I told him I was sorry but he didn't listen, didn't want to know. He must have been dead mad.

Sometimes, I'd see him around, across the street or walking into a shop. But by the time I caught up with him it was someone else or he had disappeared. Once I was dead certain. I ran up to him, and said, 'Hiya, Dad, where you been?' And when he turned round, it was this older bloke. No sunspecs. No Ferrari.

After that, I just left the picture on the wall and wrote DAD across the top, and WANTED across the bottom.

No luck, so I gave up looking.

Not long ago, someone took the picture down. It left a blank patch on the wall. The paint round it had faded, but the space where the picture had been was quite bright. Now that's faded too and you wouldn't know whether my dad had been there in the first place or not.

I've noticed the clouds at night often turn into animals. I've seen dragons and dinosaurs and cats and rabbits up there. They pass across the moon, dissolving and reappearing like ghosts. When I told Miss Chips about my cloud animals, she said they were phantoms.

Phantoms of the mind.

I like the idea of an animal that leaps out of your head. I also like that word – 'phantom'. Something that's there and yet not there.

One night, it looked like a dog was appearing. It had a head and ears but after a bit it disappeared. Took a sniff at the planet and didn't like the smell, Miss Chips said when I told her later.

If I had a real dog, I'd call it Star. Star's a great name for a dog. But they don't let you have animals in The House. Big Mother would go mental if she found an animal in The House.

The House is not for pets, it's for stray kids. The younger ones are below, on first and second. And below that is dining and more lavs and the rec room and workshops and Big Mother's office. She lives there. Behind her desk is a door. It's painted green, and Macker says it leads into more rooms and he's seen stairs in there so it must have bedrooms.

It's better up here than in the dorms. No one nicks your stuff. No one messes with you. Not unless you count Hodge. He messes up everyone – sooner or later. He's a braincase. He takes stuff. I've seen him. If you keep out of his way he wants to know why. If you don't, he smacks you. Some of the snot always hang around him. 'Hi, Hodgy,' they say, 'great goal. Fantastic.' Or, 'Hey, Hodge, pick us, will you. I wanna be on your team.' Of course they do. They get their head slammed else. Right heftied.

Hodge used to be a mate. We'd twock cars and burn them on the Burnwood estate. Up there, no one cared a toss. Hodge thought he was God Almighty 'cos he never got caught. And I thought I was the devil, the King of Hell, 'cos I loved the roar of fire. I liked it when there was thick smoke, and the orange flames screamed out loud. I liked the growling and the roaring. I liked it when the scarlets and the yellows jostled and wrapped round each other. I liked it when red bits broke off and flew like wings vanishing into the night. I liked feathery flames, and flames tearing each other into rags, and flames pulling down roofs and beams.

Anyway, we got careless and he got caught and given a suspended. He didn't really blame me for that. After all, to kids, being run in by the police made you a hero, Big Time.

No, what finished us was fire. I got to do a few burn-ups of my own. Small stuff, but it got around among the snot. (We called the younger kids snots 'cos everyone snivels when they first arrive at The House.) They began

8

to call me Zippo and give me chews and fags all freebie. Hodge didn't like that. The House was his patch. He didn't need a rival.

So, he set me up. It happened like this.

One Saturday, he got some cans and we went down the playing field. We were supposed to be on the coach for City's away game at Watford, but that was just an excuse not to get back to The House till late. We waited till the football lads had gone and then went behind the pavilion.

Maggot was there. He's this blobby runt who knocks around with Hodge all the time and does his nasty. They're always together: Maggot – the brains, Hodge – the heft. He's a maggot 'cos at The House he sort of feeds on the snot. He threatens them with Hodge, then squeezes them for his fag money. Anywhere else he'd be smacked flat, no sweat. But he's Hodge's pet and no one dares touch him.

Maggot had Spaz with him as usual. He's the sledge-head in Hodge's gang, big and slow. A right bouncer, a gorm, mouth always open, face always dribbling. He's that slow everyone laps him. But he can lay one on you. His brain may have gone bye-byes, but get the wrong side of his fist and he'll reconfigure your anatomy Big Time. He was a freak, like a dancing bear, and he did whatever Maggot or Hodge prodded him into.

Hodge, Maggot, Spaz. They rule, the freaks!

So, all of us were leaning against the pavilion wall having a puff when this goofy-looking kid started sounding off. He was one of Hodge's mates. He said he knew a good place for a twocking and a safe place for a burn-up. He also knew about engines and banged on about circuits and cut-outs like he was some kind of pit-stop mechanic for Ferrari. Anyway, he had a fist-sized bunch of keys he claimed could get him into anything outside an army tank. I believed him. And I didn't think it strange when Hodge said that Goofy had two lined up and that I was to drive one and they were to take the second. It was only afterwards that it struck me how dodgy the whole plan was, with four of them in one car and me in the other on my own. I should have guessed, but I'd got a bit cocky by then with all the Zippo stuff. I felt like Zorro burning tarmac, roaring into the night, always one step ahead of the sheriff.

We had to meet other end of the estate at the back of some primary school which had been closed for demolition. Local kids had smashed through the fencing, said Goofy, so you could drive over the netting and get into the playground, no sweat.

Piece of cake.

Mine was an Escort. No hubs. Tax out of date. Stank of cat pee. A good one. Goofy was straight in and handed me the key. 'Go, go,' he hissed and legged it across the road to where the others were standing beside a crappy Metro.

When I got to the school, it was in a cul-de-sac with freaking great steel railings across the road at one end.

Freaking Goofy prat. Never get stuck in a dead end. That's the number one rule. Two ways out is minimum.

A strip of waste ground separated the school from the nearest houses, so if things got bad at least we could do a runner. Unless some old sorts came out walking dogs there, we were reasonably safe.

It was very quiet, not a soul around. And not much light – kids had smashed the street lamps; obviously getting things ready for us. I found where they'd trampled down the surround netting and I bounced the Escort over the kerb, through the gap and into the playground.

I turned off the engine and let the car roll into the middle of a centre circle still showing in white on the tarmac.

Remember what I said, I was a braincase then. I must have been to believe Hodge and that goofy kid and sit in some old geezer Escort in the middle of a freaking playground for everyone to see.

But Zorro does that, puts himself on the line and that's what I was doing, no less. I was buzzing, sitting there waiting for Hodge, watching for stray kids and walkers and wondering if the owner of a clapped-out, red 1.8 Escort was missing his motor.

Anyway, I waited and waited. Nothing. No sign of the others. I wondered if they'd chickened out. But that didn't sound like Hodge. He was a nutter, but he wasn't chicken.

I decided to do the burn on my own. I began stuffing the cloth into the petrol tank, but as I got out the matches I heard the squeal of tyres, and a burst of headlights blazed the playground. A car bounced the kerb and came racing towards me. I shielded my eyes and stepped back as Hodge skidded to a halt. The doors flew open and figures emerged.

I knew then something was wrong. I knew it as soon

as they killed the lights and saw it wasn't the Metro. And I knew it when I saw it wasn't Maggot, Spaz or Goofy that surrounded me. It was four big guys.

'Keggin little snot,' said one, and I knew then it was Hodge and some of the City yobs he knows, and I'd been set up.

They gave me a right working over. A smack or two in the mouth, a few in the groin and I was biting the ground and kissing gravel.

I had a vague memory of puking up, blinding lights and revving engines before I finally passed out.

I came to, shivering, the stink of vomit filling my mouth and nostrils.

I got on to hands and knees and sicked up again.

After, I was in bed for a week.

Miss Chips says friends make the worst enemies. And she's right there. Since then Hodge has been my worst. Maggot's behind it. He was the one who fitted me up for the City Boys. He's the one spread it round I was done over. He tells Hodge how hard he is and how he can take on anybody. Hodge thinks he's the king now.

He hates me. Me and Macker are the only ones in The House who aren't scared of them. We're just careful. 'Only the mouse can tweak the lion's tail,' says Miss Chips. Sure, miss. Here, if you're mouse small and a snot and Hodge is in his den, you're the one likely to be tweaking and twitching in yer bed. Macker and I just keep out of the way if we can.

He feels sorry for Spaz, does Macker. I suppose I do too, in a way. It's no fun being a gom, a thicko, a dud-brain, a dumbo. He lets Hodge push him around because he's scared of him.

But one day Hodge will push too hard, and Spaz will lay one on him, and that'll be starlights and kissing tarmac for Hodgy-boy.

2

Star

I went to Science Club once and saw the Milky Way with Dimmo. He has this telescope – he's the teacher – and it's mental, brilliant. Trillions of stars in a misty swirl. Dimmo told us it only looked milky. According to him stars are just gas. They look electric to me; little fizzles like Christmas tree lights, only smaller.

Gnat lights.

And that's when I first saw Star, as I lay in bed looking up through the window at the blue-black night and the chalky-white moon. I had been awake for longer than usual. The last of the ghost clouds drifted past and then all I could see was the endless ocean of the night, a-fizzle with stars by the billion.

Bit by bit, the wind began to whisper and I realized it had been quietly breathing in the trees outside my room for some time. It was sniffing the leaves, and occasionally growling and gasping like a dog pulling on a lead. I listened to its voice deepening all the time as it shouldered through the branches and batted its forehead against the glass of my window.

I pulled up the bedclothes, tucked them tight round

my neck and watched the sky. The ghost clouds had returned. They were streaming in from every side now (Dimmo says there are no sides in space, which I don't understand) and gathering in front of the moon as if it was holding them there by some invisible force. You think I was imagining this? That it didn't really happen? Well, I say anything is possible in space. There are forces and strange things out there that we don't really understand. For instance, Dimmo says time bends and that if we fell into a black hole we'd all stretch into long strings like spaghetti. Even Fat Fat Jane would be pasta faster than you could say tart. But not me. I've got my mate, gravity. He keeps my feet on the ground and m'body tucked up tight in bed.

Even so, I know, looking back, that something strange happened that night, and it wasn't just my imagination.

Because this was the night I watched Star being born.

Up in the heavens, I saw something that had my heart drum-rolling. Round the moon, now as big as a pudding basin, the cloud drift had thickened and out of the swirling smoke I saw a dark form taking shape. I watched, gob-smacked. First came the muzzle, twitching and sniff sniffing. Then ears flicked up and a mouth opened and teeth edged out. The whole head followed, dragging out the rest of the body – chest, the long back, the haunches, the legs, the big, soft paws.

The back paw shook off the last clot of cloud and the animal looked around.

It was huge. A giant dog with a dog bowl moon.

I stared and stared.

Then a swirl threaded and wrapped itself into a flying

tail. One swish would have scattered a billion stars. A trillion even.

I couldn't move. I could hardly breathe.

Then slowly it turned its beautiful eyes on me and gazed down.

I'll call you Star, I whispered. Star shall be your name.

Then it roared and rattled the windows. It was saying, yes. The sound must have dizzied the stars, spun the planets.

I know Dimmo says sound waves don't travel in space but he's wrong on that one. Star's first word leapfrogged light and it went echoing round and round the Milky Way.

Another roar.

I sat up with a jolt. The clouds were fading. Star had turned and was moving into the vast darknesses where he belonged, where he roamed and hunted.

Soon I would be at his side. We would walk together. He and I.

I drifted into deep space, trying to avoid the black holes and keep up with Star.

Another reason I like it up here on the top floor is because you can hear the mice. Scratching and scuffling in the ceiling. Big Mother gets in the catcher but they always come back. Not even Big Mother can get rid of mice. I like that. Long live mice. I saw a nest of them once, in the graveyard, in the long grass. Little pink rubbery things.

Maybe mice listen to us. Watch us through little holes. Look at us running and skittering about, pink blind squeakers like them, only bigger. Squeak. Squeak. Look at our big brothers. Squeak.

Now, at this minute, I'm not listening for mice or for Hodge or for the water in the pipes. I'm waiting for her. For Big Mother. Every night you can hear her coming up. Every night. Coming to visit.

The steps creak.

At the top, she stops. She's listening. Like a cat on the prowl, waiting for silly mice to betray themselves.

Now she is coming. Soft steps and the slow tap tap on the radiator. Tap. Tap. Tap. The Hand. The Hand. The Hand is tapping out its warning. Be in bed. Be still. Beware.

Every night. I count the steps. Eight, nine and ten. She's outside the door. She stops. The curtains are open. I can see the stars. I'm as still as the stars. Not moving. Hardly breathing. I know she's there. She waits. I wait. I hear the *sshh* of the wind. I hear my heart deep inside me pit-a-pattering like a running rabbit in a tunnel.

Sometimes, she opens the door. Very slowly, and stands there. I pull up the sheets and wish Star was in the room. He'd growl like dogs do when they sense Bad Things near. She'd back off. She'd know she'd met her match.

At night she has no eyes. Just a mouth. A black hole of a mouth. Very faint is her breathing. She is sucking out my air, blowing darkness back into my room like it is gas. She is trying to stifle me.

My lungs are collapsing. I gasp for life.

I am breathing in the air of her.

17

I watch the dark, eyes wide, seeing nothing.

I listen. I can hear the hush hush of the breeze outside.

The Hand has gone.

She has gone, the nightmare.

And I'm OK. I'm breathing again.

She has moved on. She must have reached Macker's room by now.

Macker spills things and he looks a freak. Bits of his hair stick up. He only has bits because the rest is bald. Patches of bald skin where something is wrong and the hair won't grow. It's been like this for the last few months. No one knows the reason. Mac never hurt anyone. He's just sloppy. He used to grin a lot, but he doesn't now so much. There is no Bad Thing in Macker like there's a Bad Thing in Hodge and Maggot and Spaz and Big Mother.

No Bad Thing in Mac.

And when I'm thinking this, I get to thinking about burning again. And about how I want to flame The House and everything in it. I want to burn out the Bad Thing. Burn it out, every bit. I want raw fire, turning everything to gold and red.

And I know it's a Bad Thing, wanting to destroy The House. But sometimes it takes a second Bad Thing to get rid of the first.

I drift into sleep. Dark flames wag at me and dead men's fingers tap at the window. I wake in a sweat. The wake-up snot is banging on the door. I turn over and look out at the weather. It is raining. It is Sunday and it is porridge.

*

We're outside the dining room, lined up and waiting inspection. I'm wiping my toe caps on the back of my trousers; rubbing them up and down to get a bit of a shine. We have to be clean and combed, and ties have to cover top shirt buttons. Or else.

No mank under nails. No mank down ear-holes. No mank anywhere.

God has made us mankless. Big Mother aims to keep it that way.

Dirty body, dirty mind, she says.

Mank in yer hair, mank in yer soul.

It's dark in the corridor. I can smell polish and the mank of kitchen – steamed dishcloth and burnt porridge.

The swing doors open. We parade in, silent, heads bowed, hands to one side, and as we pass Big M we flip them over from palm to knuckle-side up.

Macker's through – surprise, surprise! Me too. But then, I skin-bite my nails, keep them below dirt level.

'Filthy.'

Two of the snot are sent back.

'Get washed.'

After Thank God Grace, Big Mother says: 'Good! Only two little filths today. Remember – dirty body, dirty mind. This is a clean house. I want it kept that way. Don't forget. Now, sit.'

We sit.

Hodge used to say that all this stuff about shine and clean was a load of mank. When you're from the bottom of the barrel you're always mank, some way or other.

That's what Big Mother really thinks. He said he was outside her office once and he heard her say the bit about barrels to dim Dave, the prat from Social Services, the SS. I'd rather be at the bottom of the barrel than be in Big Mother's pocket like Dave the dim.

As we wait for the porridge pots to arrive we have to listen to another Big Blah, this time about The House and how we're all one family.

Yes, Big Mother is saying, we're all her Family. Her Children. She does it all for us. We must not forget that. She sees we are warm. She gives us to drink. She gives us to eat.

This is what Big Mother tells us at breakfast. Today and every day. It's a sort of prayer. She tells us to be thankful we belong to a Big Family. Big Families are better than little ones. We are to be thankful we don't have to sleep outside in the cold like some children in Africa and things. We are to be thankful we have something warm to eat.

By the time I get my porridge it's cold. That's because Hodge is serving and I've had to wait till last. This is how things happen here.

I spit out the first spoonful. Someone has dosed it with salt. Buckets of it.

Bad luck for me, Big Mother sees the flying gob of porridge. Before you can say Happy Families she strides over and grabs me. I can see the spit of anger gathering on her fat lips. In her good hand she has a wooden spoon. She holds on to my wrist and cracks the spoon down and across my knuckles. 'You . . . (CRACK) . . . disgusting . . . (CRACK) . . . little . . . (CRACK) . . . pig . . .

(CRACK) . . . pig, pig, pig.' She finishes with a tattoo and a clout to the head like I was some kind of drum kit. 'Filthy! Filthy. Filthy.'

I am forced to eat. She pushes my face down with the Hand. The bowl smells like wet towels. I try to breathe through my mouth.

No one speaks.

They are all looking at me. I glance from one side to the other. Macker's eyes are wide. He is terrified. Hodge and Maggot are smiling. Spaz is grinning. I grip the metal spoon. My knuckles sting. I know I am going to be sick. I know I am going to puke salt porridge everywhere. My shoulders heave. Big Mother moves out of range. Kids back off. The nearest get up. Pretend they've finished.

I lift the spoon. The grey stuff sits in the bowl of the spoon. It is the colour of dead toad, bulgy, slimy.

I raise the spoon and vomit.

I have to mop it up. I'm 'filth' and have to clean up my own mess. One of the kitchen women slaps the wet cloth on the table in front of me. She stands over me like a Big Mother, arms folded and eyes shrunk and tight. 'Good food wasted.' The words sound like gas is hissing out of her mouth.

What about all those Africans, she says, as if it's my fault they're starving. You'd have to be hungry to death to eat this muck, I think as I smear the splatters of porridge with my first wipe. I imagine a boatload of porridge, a giant tanker full of it bound for Africa. I think of those black kids and their porridge-pot bellies.

Big Mother's right. I'm glad I'm not like them, fat with hunger.

I have to see Big Mother after school, in her office. Tomorrow! Sunday's her day off. I'll get the Hand for this, I know it. She won't forget. She never forgets.

After breakfast, Macker and I decide to go to Chuffer's hut.

We're standing by the allotment gate. Macker hasn't said a word for ages and I'm beginning to regret asking him to come. He has been a bit moody lately. Suddenly he starts giving the gate a good kicking, and as I watch him I realize how big he's getting. It seems that overnight he's grown like one of Chuffer's marrows.

Then he stops. 'One day,' he says, 'I'm going to do Hodge in.'

Do Hodge in? Come off it, Mac. Are you joking? Mince Hodge? You couldn't mash marrow. Big you may be, but you haven't got the up for it. Just to touch Hodge, you've got to be hard inside.

'It's a bad thing, Jez, when brickheads rule,' he says.

I nod. 'He's in,' I say.

We stop and look across Chuffer's patch towards his hut. Grey smoke is pouring out of the chimney pipe and rolling low over weeds and empty cold frames and yellowing potato plants. These are Chuffer's 'Lates', specially grown for winter use. He'd dig up a few big ones, wrap them in foil and put them in the top of the stove for an hour. Then he'd slice them in half like two boats and mash in some marge. Then he'd spoon out the goodness as he called it and give the skins to us sometimes.

Just now, my mouth full of puke breath, I'd give anything for one of Chuffer's spuds. I can see it all. The mash in its crisp of skin, warm and glistening with yellow fat.

Chuffer used to work on the railways. He was a loco driver when trains ran on chuff. 'And on time,' he used to say. 'Steam's the stuff. Doesn't let yer down. Lectricity's not the same. You can't smell it for a start. Can't hear it. Can't see it. Don't trust what you can't see, can't feel. Right, lads?'

We just used to nod.

Chuffer was OK. He said schools were a waste of time. They were OK for education, but no good for anything useful like fixing a broken valve-rod. He never learnt a thing as a kid. 'Look at me, I've got m'hut and m'baccy and m'beans. What more could you want?'

Macker and I never said anything when Chuffer talked like this. We just looked at his manky yellow sprouts and his shrivelled beans and wondered and wondered, what more, what more!

Afterwards, Macker wanted to know if our future was more than baccy and beans.

'Dunno,' I said. 'Maybe if we got an education we'd find out.'

The hut was separated into two 'rooms' by a wooden partition. The back was a storeroom, full of rusted garden tools, broken pots and collapsed compost bags. Dumped in a corner was an old rusted trunk in which

Chuffer let me stash fireworks. Near November I had this thing going with a guy on the market. He got the gear cheap at white van price and let me have wheels and rockets and thunder flashes at a giveaway cost to sell on to the school snot for Bonfire Night. I flogged the stuff half price, cash on order, and kids got the loot from Chuffer's by arrangement. I made a quiet packet. Enough for a new pair of trainers, that sort of thing.

Sometimes I delivered. But lugging fireworks around in yer backpack come November you have to be a brain-case with Hodge and crew out on the snatch for freebie Guy Fawkes goodies.

The front room of the hut was Chuffer's workshop where he spent most of his time, sitting in a large armchair suck-ing at his pipe. Smoke had yellowed his moustache and when it wiggled you knew he was in a bad mood and ready to slag off something. What he hated most were slugs, green-fly, tea bags and people who complained about all the weeds in his plot.

'Should mind their own bleedin' business,' he'd say. 'Listen, lads. It's unnatural not to have weeds. World's full of the bleeders. All this modern gardening with sprays and chemicals, it's not right. Just makes the bleeders resistant. They lap it up. Come back like monsters.'

Yes, Chuff.

We didn't argue. We weren't there to cheek old Chuffer. We were there for the warm and the stove and the smell of tired wood and dust and cobwebs and stale tobacco and the bitter taste of well-mashed tea.

The hut was a home.

3

Scragged

Usually, I try and leave The House early so I can avoid Hodge, Maggot and Spaz. I run out the back way, down the Donkey Path, along the back of the primary and up to the churchyard. It's creepy at night down the Path because there are no lights, and bushes and branches hang over and you can't see where you're putting your feet. You could tread on a rat or something.

I've seen rats in The House.

Hodge gets them. He catches them in cage traps. Then he ties their feet together and force-feeds them Coke so they swell up and go mad and thrash about. That's what Coke does to them. Then he rats some poor kid.

What he does is this. He waits till the rat is all swollen up and then he puts it, all tied up, into someone's bed. It pees everywhere and everywhere stinks. Just think. Putting your feet down the bed and then . . .

And no one dares tell Big M. Except, once I told her I had seen a rat, on the first. I looked her straight in the eye when I said this. It was true, I did see something brown run behind the Cupboard. 'I've seen a rat, Mrs Dawson,'

I told her. 'It was brown and looked unhygienic,' I said. She had the catcher in straight away.

Waste of time. No one can get rid of rats.

Today I'm on my own. Yesterday it was me got the nasty – Hodge porridge. This morning it was Macker's turn. Slugged in bed that second too long. Got himself late for inspection and Big Mother had him scrubbing out the breakfast pots manked up with burnt and grease. She's got people in the kitchen to do that but they're like her, uglies the lot, wasp you with a wet dishcloth if they got half a chance.

He'll be late for school and they'll clobber him there too. She knows that. That's why she keeps him behind. She knows kids like Macker always get it. All the teachers, especially Chadwick our headmaster, think he's out of sync. Kids wind him up. They're all forever trying to adjust him so he ticks in time with them. But Macker plays his own tune. He can't help it. Big Mother hates that, so she screws him up.

The witch.

I get to the churchyard and drop my bag and think about lighting up. There's plenty of time. School doesn't start for ages and there's no Miss Chips doing her gasping routine and banging on about how smoking stops you breathing properly. I think about trying the shed on the far side of the churchyard. I look around and stop. Down the Path I see three figures running.

Hell!

It's Hodge and the others. They're never early like this.

I scramble over the wall, drop down into nettles and run for the nearest bush.

I'm only just hidden when I hear them the other side of the wall. It sounds as though they've found something.

I peek through the leaves. I can see them looking around, up and down the path.

'Stupid little prat!' It's Maggot's voice.

'Here, give it me,' I hear Hodge say. And then they're climbing over the wall and Hodge has something in his hand.

My bag!

I hold my breathing. If they find me I'm in for a licking.

But they don't wait. Instead they dash between the stones and run for the shed. I see them disappear behind. I let out a great gasp. I'm shaking and my heart is bouncing wall to wall like a tennis ball.

Dimmo'll kill me if I turn up in Science without my homework. I try to remember what else is in the bag. Two library books, pencil case, boots.

Footic boots!

Without them I'm lost. I try to think what Hodge will want. He'll do a deal – money, fags, or bye bye boots. I'd have to nick some stuff. Do a few cars.

I decide to wait till they've gone. If that makes me late, well, then that makes me late.

It doesn't take long. Within minutes Spaz and Maggot are running up the path, urging Hodge to hurry. The churchyard is out of bounds and anyone reported will be in for a right slagging from Chadwick. Hodge isn't fussed though. Never is. No one ever reports him.

I find the bag. They've stuffed it under the shed, but the straps are showing. Bit odd, leaving the straps like that, I think.

Then, just as I'm pulling the zip, someone grabs me round the neck and jerks me back in a headlock. It must be Spaz because standing in front of me, both grinning, are Maggot and Hodge.

'Give it us.'

Maggot picks up my bag.

Hodge turns to me. 'Gotcha.' He takes hold of the zip. 'OK, Spaz, let him go.'

I stumble into Maggot, who pushes me against the shed wall. I stand there, trying to stretch the pain out of my neck. The set-up is freaking Maggot's idea probably.

'Now what have we got here? One pair niffy footie booties.' Hodge smirks. 'They need a bit of air.' And he hurls one, then the other, over his shoulder high into the holly tree behind him. 'Ooh, and homework. Little Jezzer's homework. Very neat. Dimmo's little star.' He hands the Science notebook to Maggot and tells him to copy it up, but not for Spaz.

Spaz looks all sulky. 'Why can't I have a good home-work this time? It's my turn.'

'It's never your turn, dumbo. Thickies, noddies, bazzos, goms, spazzers, dimmies, yegs don't do Science.'

Spaz says nothing. He just stands with his mouth open, head down, looking at the ground. He is breathing hard, his shoulders beginning to heave. Suddenly he turns on me and, before I know it, has me by the throat and is slamming my head against the shed. He has tears in his eyes.

'Scrag him. Give him one,' I can hear Maggot squeaking. 'One of yer specials.'

And Spaz does. He just keeps slamming me, grunting and knocking the breath out of me.

'Good one, Spaz. Scrag him, go on, the little snot.'

The voices start to fade. Spaz's face blurs. I am dizzy and everything seems distant. Maggot's voice is miles away, tiny as a mouse's. Hodge has long gone. Night falls. Everything is dark.

Black.

I wake up.

I'm on the ground and there's no one about. I try to sit up, but topple over. I feel light, almost weightless. A puff of wind would blow me into the sky. I manage to crawl over to the shed and lean my back against the wall.

I can hardly pull breath.

I am emptied.

Then gradually something wraps itself round me, gently lifts me.

I smile. I think I know who it is.

I think it's Star, come to help me. I can feel something like warm breath on my neck.

Star breath.

It is, it is Star.

I am like a pup in his huge soft mouth. He lowers me. Rolls me, stretches me. His great head nudges me upright, holds me.

His long tongue is licking life into me.

The pain begins to stretch away. Blood pump pumps. Star-growl booms in my head. My body fills up, joints tighten, muscles shift and spring back into place.

I am standing.

Strong and clear-headed.

Star is whispering in my ear. Remember, he says, next time you stand on your own two feet.

I nod. OK, OK, Star. I'll try.

Then I remember.

Spaz!

Spaz skull-banged me. Gave me some right hefties. They're still echoing.

I look round for my bag. No sign. I reach under the shed far as my arm will go and I touch something soft. It rustles in my grasp. I pull out a white plastic bag. It's knotted and something's inside. I untie it and out tumble a load of little white pills. These aren't aspirin. It's Hodge's stash of E. I count over two hundred. Nice money.

I start thinking. Nice scam, Hodge, but not for long.

An idea begins to form. And the more I think about it, the more I like it. I smile to myself. This will be something Hodge won't forget.

I return the pills, knot the bag and push it back, right back where I found it.

At the edge of the churchyard, I stop, turn, and look at the shed. It's grafittied in bird poo and the roof felt's peeling away.

It needs a good burning.

I'm still a bit giddy, so I go and sit in the church porch and wonder whether to bunk off. I check my watch. It's past nine and I'm already twenty minutes late. It's then I realize how long I've been out. Dunked unconscious for half an hour. He could have killed me. He needs a head transplant, that Spaz freak.

I decide to wait till the end of the first lesson and then slip in the back way, past the boiler house during the changeover when everyone is rushing about. Then, at dinnertime, I'll have to find Miss Chips and make up some story or other. I don't like putting one over Miss Chips because she's OK. She's got dead-black hair and smiles a lot. She smells nice and looks nice. Her real name is Chipanowicz. Now you see why we call her Chips. Hodge is always trying to chat her up, and sits on her table at dinnertime. He fancies her. Once he told her she was top shelf, whatever that means. I don't think she liked him saying that. She'll give me a note for Dimmo this afternoon. He won't believe a word.

Outside the porch, I look up at the church tower. At the top corners, the gargoyles look smoothed and worn almost faceless. Like skinned rabbits.

Above, in the blue sky, crows – I think they're crows – take off, screaming. It's windy. They are being tossed about and look like the black scraps you see rising from bonfires.

Almost touching the porch are the lower branches of a gigantic oak tree. That's where I'd stash the E, not under some manky shed. From the ground, you can see lots of holes and cracks in the bark. At the bottom, near the roots, there are rabbit holes. Put the stuff down there and bunnies would be hopping all night.

It may be sunny, but it's bum cold out and I return to the porch. On the stone floor, tucked under the bench facing me, is a dead bird. Its wings are folded, its bright eye closed. It looks like a little boat on its side cast against a harbour wall, huddled up.

I think about my dad again. He's not been around for a bit. But today he's back, in my mind. Very close.

Back then, after I had been searching all over, I realized, bit by bit, he wasn't going to come back. Maybe I was eight, maybe nine at the time. Just a kid. One day I decided he had died. That was why I couldn't find him. He'd died. That's why he hadn't come to collect me, take me home. I didn't feel bad about it. I know I should have cried my little heart out. But when you're a kid a dead dad is better than no dad in the first place, and it was a relief to know he wasn't just avoiding me, that he didn't care any more.

I knew he must be buried somewhere, so I decided to look for him. That's when I started going to church-yards. I used to come to this place and wander round, inspecting the stones, reading the names and the dates. People, mainly oldies, used to ask me what I thought I was doing. I said I was looking for my father. They'd say sorry, or pat me on the head or give me a coin or two, manky pennies mostly. Then they left me.

I couldn't find a Walker anywhere. Anyway, they're all old graves in this place. If Dad was dead he'd be in a new one somewhere. Back then, I didn't cotton on to

32

this. I probably thought you just lifted the stone lid and popped in the body.

I used to wonder what Dad looked like. He probably just huddled up in the end.

It's sad really. We had so many plans.

If he was here now, we could go off somewhere, like he used to say. Forget Chips and The House and Hodge and Big Mother and just go, down to the bus stop, get the first one and see where it went. Or a train. A train up to Scotland. Up there it's wild, full of mountains and eagles. We could camp out and fish, and Dad would trap rabbits and things. We could make fires out of dead wood and he'd cook them on a spit. We'd get eggs from farmers and milk and we'd lie awake at night listening to otters barking and watching the stars.

I look at the dead bird lying on the cold stone. Will the sun warm it back to life again? Will it fly once more?

No way.

But I go over to where it lies and kneel beside it. As I turn the body over to scoop it up, a white maggot drops out. It wriggles and wriggles.

I run out into the cold sunshine, wiping my hand on my trousers.

Sick rises.

I race on to the Donkey Path.

And STOP.

Front of me's this hawthorn bush. Massive thing.

Two metres up, looking like it had just dropped out of the sky, is my bag.

I shake it down.

It's empty. Books, pencil case, all gone.

The goms!

Miss Chips'll earbash me for this.

Then I sniff something.

Then I notice the bag's all wet down one side.

Then I lift it up a bit.

Sniff again.

Rat pee?

No, Dog.

No, not Dog.

Jiggin Spaz pee.

And Maggot pee.

And Hodge pee.

Filth. Bastards!

I give the bag a right kicking like I'm giving Spaz a one–two in the groin. I stamp on it like it's Hodge's face I'm flat-packing. I stamp and stamp till it's trashed and muddied and you couldn't even recognize it as human, never mind Hodge. Then I grab a handle, whirl the whole thing round my head and fling it high as I can, high over the hawthorn and out of sight like I'm trying to hurl all the freak and the mank out of my life.

I turn, breathing a bit heavy, and walk towards school.

I start working out how I'm going to fix it with Miss Chips, especially about the books. She makes out tough at times because she's our form teacher and has to keep us in line, but she has a soft bit inside. I think she feels sorry for me coming from a home and that. I once told her about my dad. That was one time she put her arm round me. An almost hug.

I think my dad would be good at hugging. Maybe he'll sort it out with Miss C. If I mention him, just in passing like, maybe she won't go tough on me. Maybe she'll soften up. Maybe I'll get another bag, from Lost Property, compliment of Miss C.

Maybe I will.

4

Getting the Hand

I'm now sitting in Dimmo's lesson, watching the bunsen flame heating the test tube. We've got to observe the substance in there and say what happens after one minute, after two, after three. Macker has the stopwatch, I'm in charge of the glass tube and Fat Fat Jane is recording our observations.

'What's supposed to happen?' says Macker.

'Just watch.'

'But what's the point?'

'Point of what?'

'Watching.'

'Stops you walking into a wall.'

'No, I mean why watch this stuff.'

''Cos we might learn something.'

'Like what?'

'Like what's in this tube, dumbo,' says Fat Fat Jane. 'Don't you ever listen?' She has a small make-up mirror out and is angling it so she can watch Matt Thomas on the bench behind us.

'And then what?'

'And then we can go home,' she says, pursing her big lips at the mirror in a slow red kiss.

Zit-face Thomas. Wozzeck.

It turns out Macker has forgotten to set the watch. So we have to start all over again. I switch off the burner and tell Dimmo. He says to carry on. I tell him the bunsen needs re-lighting and can I get the taper. I know the tapers are in his desk, top drawer with the matches. He's busy, so he says yes. I get the taper and slip a matchbox in my pocket. It's that easy.

Back at the bench, Fat Fat Jane is filling a hole in her tights with felt tip and Macker has some dried nose picks on paper ready for burning.

I borrow a light and set our bunsen off. I watch the flame. It divides into little hands, cupping and stroking the glass. Then they seem to change into misty petals, purple one minute, blue the next.

'That's a minute,' says Macker

We look at the test tube. It looks the same – dirty grey. Fat Fat Jane writes, 'dirty grey'.

At two minutes it's still the same. Same after three minutes. We're puzzled. No change. Why?

'The watch could be slow,' suggests Macker.

'Like you,' says Fat Fat Jane. 'What's the watch got to do with it?'

'I mean we're not giving it enough time.' Macker's used to being called by Fat Fat Jane. She calls everyone.

Suddenly, Dimmo is shouting. He wants to know immediately the identity of the person who has opened the stink cupboard. Everyone starts coughing. Dimmo is shouting again. If we don't stop coughing, we're all in detention. We all stop coughing.

'Always the same,' says Macker. 'The same old same, again!'

I look at him, sniffing and dribbling a bit, and wonder if he's going loopy.

Next it's History. Room 8P, Floor 1 with Miss Chips. She's our form teacher and she takes us for History. She calls it hands-on History. She says it's about what gets left behind after time has passed by. She says History's like a broken pot. We find a few bits here and there and History adds a few more and puts them together to see what the original was like. It's like doing a jigsaw puzzle where you have to make up your own picture, she says. I don't understand this really, but it sounds right. Lots of things Miss Chips says sound right; that's why she's a good teacher.

Today, Miss Chips says we are starting a new project, working in pairs. I hate pairs. I could get Fat Fat Jane. If I do, I'll do a swap and ask to be with Macker. It won't happen. We have to be mixed. Girl and Boy. I hate working with girls. They write too much. They're always writing.

Miss Chips says Macker and I are soul mates. I tell her we're just mates, we always have been ever since we had beds next to each other in the snot dorm. 'Snot?' she frowns. I explain. 'At The House, that's what we call little uns, the snot.'

She nods slowly and just mouths the word as if it's something mank she doesn't want to touch, like a slug or something. 'Ah ha,' she goes, like at the doctor's when he looks down your throat. She's nice, but a bit posh, is Miss Chips. Bit lah-di-dah. But she's a teacher so it's all right.

'It's 'cos they're always snivelling and dribbling,' sniffs Macker. But she doesn't hear. She's moved off.

Yes, we sit together, all the time, Macker and me, but it's not like it used to be. He's changed a bit. You ask him a question about United or something and he just shrugs like he's not interested, like it's nothing to do with him, like he's given up. He used to be mad about United. And sometimes when I catch his eye, accidental-like, he looks away from you like he's been caught out or like he's hiding something.

It must be a mood swing. We did that in Personal Education, hormones and stuff. It's not just for girls. Boys get it too. Even teachers. Everyone gets it. Macker more than most maybe.

Anyway, Miss C is pairing us off.

I don't get Fat Fat Jane. I don't get Loosey Lucy. I get Mags Wilkinson. Wee Willa Wilko. A dimbo!

I turn round and look across the room to where Wilkinson sits. She's not as little as I thought. She must have grown recently. She gives me a bit of a smile and a shrug. Is that an 'OK' shrug? Is that an 'I couldn't care less' shrug? Is that a 'let's wait and see' shrug? Is that an 'I'll do it if I have to' shrug?

Well, same to you Wilko, and I turn my back.

Next thing I know, she's standing beside me and telling me to move over. She smells of soap. Not the sort you get at The House in the lavs. It's more like the stuff you get in those posh shops up town like Boots.

Then she sits down and starts sharpening my pencil. It's all I've got after Hodge nicked my bag.

I grab the pencil off her. It's mine. I give her a right frowning.

She gets up and goes back to her place. She puts up her hand and Miss Chips asks her what she wants.

She wants to change partners. She wants to work on her own. She doesn't want to work with a stupid boy. Especially Jez Walker. She says my name slowly, pushing her head back as if she's about to sick it up.

No one says anything. Fat Fat Jane giggles and gives me the finger. I make to gob at her. She's a cow.

So is Wilko. What's she playing at? What's wrong with me? If it's my pencil it's my pencil. What right's she got to go sharpening it? I'll decide when it gets a good sharpen.

Macker volunteers to work with me but Miss C is having no messing about.

She calls me to her desk. Everyone else is to read the worksheets Loosey Lucy is handing out.

Miss C says I can help Mags Wilkinson. I'm hot on words. She isn't.

'So she's a dimbo,' I say.

'No one's a dimbo,' snaps Miss C. 'Mags has a different way of looking at things. She's very sensitive.'

So I've got to play puffy with a dimbo.

I don't say this. I say I'm sensitive too and she

shouldn't try and run my life and sharpen my pencils.

Miss C makes me promise I'll help.

I promise. But only because it's Miss Chips.

I sit down.

She calls Wilko to her desk.

I watch them talk and for the first time I take notice of Wilko. She's got blonde hair and it's tied up at the back like a horse's tail. Her sleeves are too short for her arms and she's a bit thin and not very developed. She doesn't look like a dimbo. She's nodding and shrugging and waving her hands a bit.

Then she looks over to me. Smiles.

I smile back but let it fade quickly. I know about smiling. In The House, when you're a snot you smile a lot, or else. Later you want to be hard, so smiles are out. Only snots smile.

Miss C calls me back to her desk. 'You two are going to be a great team,' she says.

Wilko nods. I nod too. I hear someone give a low whistle. I know it's Fat Fat Jane, the cow. One day I'll kick her downstairs.

The project is about old buildings. We have to choose one to study from a list in front of us. I read out the names slowly. St Bertoline's Church, Fenwicks Brewery, Mill End Almshouses, the Methodist School and Chapel, the Old Hospital and Apothecary's Shop, Central Station, the Rope Factory, the Odeon Cinema.

Naturally, we can't agree. No surprise! She wants the

church because it has the most history. I want the Odeon because it has the least history.

We sit there in silence. Dumb and dim together.

After a bit, Wilko opens a green pencil case. It's stashed full of pencils. Hundreds of them. All sharpened. Missile battery. She's a pencil freak. I'm sitting next to a nutter. She pulls one out slow like it's made of glass. It's only a dumb pencil after all. She twizzles it, strokes it and then suddenly dives on to the paper.

I pretend I'm not watching. In seconds she's drawn a bird. It's flying, on the turn, one wing shorter as it swings right. She draws another and another, dead quick, no pause, till there's a whole freaking flock of them skimming across the paper and over the printed words.

Suddenly Miss Chips is standing next to us.

'We can't agree,' says Wilko. 'He wants the cinema. I want the church.'

'Toss for it,' I say.

Miss Chips ignores the birds and gives me one of her looks.

'OK,' I say. 'We'll do the church if that's what you want.'

Wilko stares at me.

'No. We'll do the Odeon.'

'Toss for it,' I say with a bit of a smile.

Miss Chips throws up her arms and walks off.

At break, I look round for Hodge. I want my books and stuff back. But there's no sign of any of them. I wonder, should I have told Miss Chips about him? Maybe not. If he found out I'd snotted on him, I'd get a right doing over.

At the bell for end of lessons, I get out of school quick. I double check. I've got Dimmos's taper and a full box of matches stuffing my inside parka pocket. I've talked to Macker. He'll let me use his window. 'Burn the whole dimmo town down,' he says. 'No way, Macker,' says I. 'You need a volcano for that, not a packet of Swan Vestas.'

I start walking back to The House, eyeing the dark clouds and hoping it won't rain. I'm so full of the thinking and planning I don't notice the figure standing beside the fence at the entrance to the Donkey Path.

'Hi, Walker.'

It's Wilko.

'You live at the home, don't you?' she says.

'Yeah, so what.'

'So, that's tough.'

I shrug.

Wilko is looking at me sideways like she doesn't trust me, like I might do something off the wall, like I was mental or something.

Then she turns away and says: 'I don't have a dad either, you know.'

'Oh!'

'So, you're not the only one.' She turns again and looks me in the eye. Is she giving sympathy or is she after it?

'But you've got a mum, haven't you?' I say.

She frowns. 'It's not like having a dad though, is it?'

I shrug. How should I know?

'So, we're both in the same boat,' she says.

I look at her. I suddenly realize she's taller than me. And it can't be high heels or anything because she's wearing flat dancing pumps as Miss Chips calls them. No, we're not in the same boat.

'Well, you're wrong,' I say. 'I do have a dad.'

She frowns. 'So, why are you in a home?'

'He's away at the moment. Travelling. In Australia.'

It is a lie, of course. And I think Wilko knows it. As soon as I say it, I wish I hadn't. Now it seems like the biggest lie in the whole world, bigger than Australia even. I can still hear the words in my mouth and they taste of dust and gravel.

'Australia?' She pauses. 'Mine's away as well.'

We swap glances.

'You mean . . .?'

Wilko nods.

'Has he been away a long time?'

She nods again.

'Long, long time?'

More nods. Very slow.

'Mine too. But he'll be back one day.'

Wilko hums doubtfully and looks at me like I need advice or something. 'Mine won't. My mum says they never come back. I don't think dads are all they're cracked up to be. When did you last see yours?'

'Dunno. But I've got his picture.'

Not even this is true any more. There's just that big wide-open space now where my dad used to be. I begin to wonder. Should you pretend or should you let the

44

truth get the better of you? Trouble is, you can't lean on the truth. It's a pain.

'Picture?' Wilko is saying. She is opening her backpack, which up to now has been clutched across her chest.

'I've done a drawing,' she says. 'It's the home. You can have it if you want.' She tears a piece of paper off a writing pad and holds it out.

I take it. It's a sketch of The House. One side is coloured a light brown, and green ivy sweeps up the wall and over part of the roof. Grey smoke drifts out of one of the five chimneys. She's put roses in the garden.

'It's not like that,' I say. 'It's a dump.'

'Oh!'

'A right keggin dump!'

'It looks OK to me.'

'Well, you don't have to live there, do you! It's a nightmare.'

'You don't have to shout. It's not my fault you're in there. I was only trying to help,' she says, turning.

'I don't need any help. And I don't need any crappy doodles either.'

She looks at me, shock stiffening her face. I suddenly feel bad.

'They don't let you put up pictures any more,' I mumble.

'I'm not surprised,' she says. 'You're pig ignorant.' She says 'pig' like she's gobbing spit at me. She shoves the pad into her backpack, snaps the flap shut and flings it over her shoulder. 'Pig ignorant,' she says, walking away.

'No I am not,' I shout, suddenly mad again. 'I had a

picture once. A real picture. Of my dad. It was great. Now it's gone. But what would you know? You're a posh tart.'

She stops and slowly turns round. Then she walks up to me dead close, close enough for me to smell soap, and says very quietly: 'My dad's not in Australia. He's dead.'

Hell!

She turns.

I watch her go. Her head is bowed and I can see that her shoulders are heaving. I suppose she is crying.

Hell! All because of some crappy drawing. I crumple the paper and jam it into my pocket.

Now, we'll have to do the church.

When I get back to The House, Big Mother's waiting for me. She's standing in the hallway, the right arm, the one with the Hand, behind her back. That's where it's always kept, out of sight, like a threat.

She points to her office and I walk down the corridor. I can hear her breathing, quick and slightly hoarse. We get to her door and she leans over my shoulder and turns the handle. I'm pushed in.

'On the stool.'

This is a high wooden thing. I climb up, sit on the top, my feet dangling. Big Mother puts her toe against one of the legs and pushes. The stool starts to wobble. I grip the seat. She removes her foot.

'So, you think spitting porridge is fun?'

'No, no, Mrs Dawson. It was salty. It made me sick.'

'Made you sick? Nobody else was sick. Why did it have to be you? Why is it always you?'

'It wasn't me. Someone put salt in it. Lots of salt.'

'That's it, blame somebody else. Good food doesn't make you sick. There are people here night and day working to give you decent food. No fancy rubbish in my house. You were just trying to cause trouble as usual. I know your type. Always spoiling it for others.'

She shoves her foot hard against the stool. It tilts. She pushes harder. I begin to slide. I reach out, my arms flailing. I grab something. It's Big Mother and I'm gripping her shoulder.

'Let go,' she hisses. 'Get your hands off. Don't you touch me, you filthy little animal! How dare you attack me? I'll teach you something you won't forget.'

She seizes my arm, steadies me, and holds on as if lining me up for a clout. My heart is racing. Then, from behind her back she brings it out.

The Hand.

The wooden one. Usually the fingers are curled up like they are asleep. She pulls at a lever hidden under her sleeve and the fingers open up, straight and wide like cat's claws. She squeezes the four wooden fingers and they click together, flat.

'Hold it out, palm up. Quick. I haven't got all day.'

I put out my hand.

'Higher.'

I raise it.

SMACK.

My fingers curl up. The skin's on fire. The pain pulses deeper and deeper through the soft bits and into the bone. I am trembling.

'Other one.'

My left hand stutters out.

She grabs it, forces the fingers straight, yanks the arm.

I watch the Hand rise. She holds it high. I close my eyes. Screw them up. Then swish . . . ish . . . ish.

SMACK.

Puke rises. My throat closes. I can't breathe. Everything is hazy. Someone is grabbing me. My hands are squeezed in pain.

I am on the floor. Big Mother is standing over me.

'It's for your own good, boy. We've got to have discipline. Now, get up and stop snivelling.'

Back in bed, I have a wet towel wrapped round my hands. Macker says this helps the stinging. He should know. He's had the Hand more than me. He says she takes it off at night and hangs it up beside her bed. Her real arm stops at the elbow. He says a tiger bit off the rest. That's typical Macker, that story. He's a nutcase. She was probably born like that, a one-off freak from the beginning.

Today, in Miss Chips' class, I thought I heard Star in my head, whispering to me, inside. Probably he was just checking me out; seeing I was OK after Spaz head-banged me in the churchyard. But that's just my imagination. Most likely he sleeps during the day, curled up, curled up inside me maybe.

I think he's there all the time but doesn't let on. He sort of hides and just watches without me knowing. I wonder how long he's been around? Was he there when my dad left? Was it then he started looking out for me?

I bet he follows me to school. If I keep turning round dead quick, one day I could catch him out before he hides. Fat chance!

He's too fast really. Too clever. Too sharp.

It's only at night you can see Star.

I'm looking through the window but it's cloudy. I know he's out there somewhere. I can feel him listening. I ask him if he knows anything about the Hand. He says some people are born with bits missing. It's life. It's tough.

No need to take it out on kids, I say.

I tell him I hate Big Mother and The House and Hodge and the lot. He says it's OK to be angry, but not OK to hate. I say, what's the difference, hate or anger? Anger is hot, he says, but like fire you can put it out and stop it burning. Hate is cold, like a stone; it never dies.

'Well, I still want to kill her, whatever you say.'

'Well,' says Star, 'we're certainly going to have to do something about her.'

5

Torching

I'm thinking about Mags Wilkinson and her dad. At least mine's out there somewhere and one day, one day I might meet him. But it's not like that with Mags. She's no chance. That's it. Gone. The space will always be blank for Mags now.

Bad Thing Big Time.

Maybe he's buried in the churchyard. That's why she was hanging around the Donkey Path. Maybe she goes to talk to him. A girl would do that sort of thing. They believe in ghosts. Not me. No way.

I feel a Bad Thing inside me about her picture and all. But I didn't ask her to do one. Maybe I will next time. Maybe I'll let her draw Star – one day, eh!

You hear that, Star, I say, looking up through the window into the starry night.

If I sit up I can see a square chimneystack rising above the roof ridge and grey clouds rushing beyond. Sometimes they look like they're streaming from the chimney pot, flattened and thinned by wind.

I want Star to stop the moonlight. I want it soot-black

for my fire. Jump for the moon, Star. Catch it. Run away with it.

I am slowly bending my fingers. It hurts but I feel that if I do this I will squeeze out the pain. It's hard because my hands are hot and feel tight. But it's not going to stop me. Not tonight.

Someone's just given my door a hefty. Has to be Hodge on his way back from the first lavs. I heard them at supper, planning a wasping for some of the snot for getting out of line, he and Spaz. What they do is get some snot starkers, cold him under a shower so it hurts more, and then flick him with wet towels till he's stung red all over. The freaks, it really burns you.

Macker's up for it tonight.

He'll leave the window open till I get back.

Under the sheets, I'm all dressed – tracksuit, trainers. Trainers are quiet. I check the kit. Matches, can, Dimmo's taper.

Sorted.

Big Mother has passed. I heard the Hand. I heard the breathing. I saw her shadow. I waited, watching the crowded sky. There was no sign of Star.

Now it's time.

I'll be going out through Macker's window on to the fire escape. It zigzags all the way down to the bottom. I've done it before. It's no big deal. There's a ladder bit you have to lower to the ground at the end. The drop's about two metres. Enough to break your leg if you jump, especially in the dark.

I'm hoping for wind tonight. It drives fire mad.

It's good and dark all the way, through the garden, down the Donkey Path and across the churchyard. Still, I don't want any moon. Just keep out of my way, moon.

I slip out of bed. By the door, I stop and lean into the corridor. Not a sound. I tiptoe out. I know which boards creak, which dip and rise. I round the corner and see the night light outside Macker's room. His door's open.

I'm about five metres away when I hear it. Tap. Tap. Tap.

I freeze.

The Hand. Big Mother. She's coming back. Has she heard me? Does she know something?

Tap. Tap. Tap.

I dash for Macker's and burst into the darkness.

'It's me,' I hiss, and Macker sighs. A shadow passes across the half-open doorway. I lower myself slowly, slowly below the far side of the bed. Macker starts his snores, putting it on, each snarly and growly, double-barrelled beauties.

I sit there, listening.

I peep over the bed. Is she there? I listen, listen. Macker stops.

Slowly the door opens.

It scrapes across the carpet, like a long, long hoarse breath. I flatten myself on the floor and half edge under the bed.

Macker starts to snore again, quick and urgent.

She's in the room, I know. I can sense her there, standing by the bed.

I hear a rustling. The bed gives a shake. It lurches as

52

if a big weight has suddenly landed on it. More rustling.

Macker's snoring is faster and faster. His voice begins to shudder. He sounds like an exhausted runner. He is not snoring now, he is crying, a gulping, snorting crying that shakes the bed.

Suddenly it goes faint and far off, like it's under a pillow or there's a hand over his mouth.

'You filthy boy. You filthy, disgusting animal.' It's Big Mother. 'Urinating in the bed again,' she hisses.

The bedstead lurches.

'It's filthy down there.'

Then she is hitting the bed, whacking the bedclothes with the Hand and Macker is gibbering underneath. 'No. No. Please. No.'

The beating suddenly stops. Macker is still sobbing no's.

'It's for your own good,' says Big Mother and her voice becomes surprisingly quiet, almost soft. 'We can't go on like this. You have to stop it. You must stop it. This is a clean house. We can't have this sort of filth going on. I'm going to stop it. If you can't, I will. Now, come on, no more of this pathetic snivelling.'

Macker has calmed down. He has turned on his side. His head is just above me. I know he is still crying.

Through the silent tremble of his weeping I hear the door breathing over the carpet, breathing shut.

She's gone.

I'm shaking, too. Shaking for Macker, shaking for me.

Slowly I get to my knees. I lean over him. 'You OK, Macker?' I whisper.

He sniffs and grunts a yes.

'One day I'll kill the fat bitch,' I hiss.

'I didn't do it, honest. It's not my fault.'

I'm not sure what he's talking about. 'Of course not,' I say.

I feel Macker's fist give me a friendly jab.

'You're a real mate,' I say.

'Same to you,' he sniffs. 'Better go, Jez, in case she comes back.'

I hesitate.

He gives me a shove, and I taste a whiff of pee as the bedclothes rise.

'See ya in a bit,' I say and turn towards the window.

I slide behind the curtains, jack myself on to the sill, clamber out and drop soundlessly on to the metal platform outside.

I listen.

Nothing. Not a sound. That's why I use Macker's window and not the emergency door next to his room. Too noisy. Safety bar gets the dead complaining.

The air is chill. I like it sharp.

I change shape. I step like a cat. On soft pads, step after step.

The moon is watching me, peering from behind a cloud.

At the bottom, I find the ladder's been oiled and it slides easily with hardly a sound. This is a good sign. A bit of luck. Now I know it's going to be OK.

Before long I'm running, half bent, down the Donkey Path, skipping from deep shadow to deep shadow.

I roll over the churchyard wall and drop lightly into the soft wet grass. After a few moments I move forward, darting from one hunchback gravestone to another till I reach the shed.

I take out the can and put on my gloves. I shake the can. I do it under my top to kill the noise. Then I start to spray the shed, and I spray till the hissing dies and the can's empty. I'm careful. I spray away from me, at arm's length, so none of the stink gets on me. I put the top back on the can and shove it into my pocket.

I get out Dimmo's taper and the box of matches. Then I wait and listen. I go through the escape routine. I'll have a few minutes. It'll take a time before anyone around will see the flames. That's why I've started on this far side, out of view of the path. Behind, I'm shielded by the holly hedge.

I open the matchbox. My fingers are numb and I have to strike twice before I get the match to light. It is surprisingly bright. I feel the tapping of my heart. I quickly cup my hand round the laughing flame, ready to light the taper, but it blows out. I try again. And again the match dies. As I take the box out a third time, a bit of crumpled paper drops to the ground.

Mags' sketch.

I roll and twist it. Get out the can and give it the last of the spray. It flares as soon as I get a match flame near. I light the taper and drop the burning paper. Then I step back and, holding the taper at arm's length, I fire the bottom of the shed, moving round to set it alight at several points.

Like lizard tongues the flames dart into the night,

flickering and devouring each other. Soon they are every-where, skittering across the glass, a thousand tiny jaws snapping at each other's throats, hissing and snarling.

I step back from the heat and the thrashing and the snarling. I see lizards and fire rats with fat bellies of flame, growing bigger, growing and devouring. Bigger and bigger. Monster rats, monster lizards with ragged jaws roaring, roaring and crushing and slowly swallowing the hunched, black shed.

Suddenly someone is shouting. I step back, startled, and almost fall. Anyone could have seen me. I crouch down and edge into the deep shadows by the hedge.

Then I hear it – a cackling. Crazy laughter.

I look up and catch my breath.

Fire is leaping from the bush next to the shed and swinging into the giant tree in the middle of the church-yard, the King's Oak. Yes, fire is swinging and leaping like a red monkey. Yes, monkey fire chattering and racing from branch to branch. Fire, with red tails and flaming fur, laughing up there high amid the dry leaves.

I gasp and make a run for it.

I stumble through the long grass beside the hedge. I'm like a stranded salmon splashing through pools of shadow. I can see figures running down the church-yard path. They won't hear me. They only have eyes for the burning tree. When I reach the Donkey Path wall, I clamber up and slip over noiselessly. No one's around. I dash through the shadows, and don't stop till I'm back in the garden at The House.

*

56

Safe!

What a plonker! Gawping at fire like that. Well, with fire and me, it's hypnosis. It calls and I obey. It's like tripping. The world goes crazy – full of screaming red monkeys and monster lizards, each big as a tyrannosaurus.

Suddenly I realize I'm shivering. I hold one hand with the other to stop it trembling. They are both shaking. I take a deep breath. Then another.

At this moment, the moon comes out. The cloud falls away and she's there, tilted like an empty white bowl. Then I decide that's how it's going to be in future. Simple and white. Simple black and white. No more red rats and green lizards. I'm going to forget fire. Witch fire. Monkey fire.

I tiptoe towards The House wall. In a few minutes I'll be in bed, the blankets pulling the warm round my shoulders. That's the bit I like best, wrapped in your own warmth. Once I'm on the ladder it'll be easy. I'll slip through Macker's window. He'll be snoring. I imagine him dragging in air and sucking the curtain into the room. I imagine him breathing out and the curtain billowing through the window in the gust of his snores. Poor pissbed Macker.

I sidle to the corner of the building and wait for the hurrying clouds to darken the moon before I move out on to the path.

I think I hear a sound. A faint crack. Something moving. I hold my breath. Listen. Nothing. The slight rustle of leaves above. Otherwise silence.

I start on the path, feeling along the bricks, feeling for the ladder. A glimmer of moonlight washes across the face of the building and the ladder is shadowed on the wall. I pull myself on to the first rung. I sense something moving behind me. I look over my shoulder. Nothing. Only the phantom shade of trees and bushes on the grass. I pull the ladder up and slide it under the platform below.

I climb up, level by level, on tiptoe. Platform, ladder, platform, till I get to Macker's room. I clamber on to the metal grating and reach for the window.

Almost there. Almost safe.

It's closed!

Macker, what have you done, you prat?

I tap on the glass.

No answer. Tap. Tap. Tap.

Nothing.

'Macker,' I whisper, loud as I dare.

The curtains are drawn. The window stares at me blankly.

He's forgotten. Closed it by mistake.

I try again and again and again, and keep on tapping. No answer.

I sit down. I could be there all night. Till Macker wakes up.

I decide to climb down and search round and see if there's another way in. Sometimes they leave windows open in the workshop.

I get to the bottom and feel for the ladder, grab the first rung and pull.

Nothing happens.

I pull harder. Nothing. It's jammed! Whatever.

I try again. Nothing. Rock solid.

The clouds have blanked the moon. I look down. It's pit black.

I'm trapped.

Trapped!

I lean against the wall and feel something pushing into my thigh. The can. What a freaking mess! If they find this – Big Mother, the police, whoever – and the matches, I've had it. They'll know I did the fire. Up or down, I've had it.

In the moonlight I can see the rungs and the rails criss-crossing above me. I'm at the bottom of a tall cage. I'm a trapped animal. I'm like a mouse with ladders to run up and a treadmill to turn.

Well, I think, mice can escape from anything!

Then I notice a dark line, like a stripe running up the wall alongside the escape. It's a drainpipe. It's too far from me here, but at the top the platform's bigger and there the pipe could be within reach. It could lead to the roof. The roof has a skylight. It's above the lavs. It could be open. It often is . . . If it is . . . It's a chance. The only one I've got. I skitter up the ladders again, light as a mouse.

Macker's window is at the top of the escape. To the right, the floor grating ends in an expanded metal wall that rises about two metres then curves round and back over the platform so it looks like a cage. To the left, I can see the dark shape of the emergency door. I clamber on to the metal flooring. OK, this is an emergency so I try the door. Solid. Solid as a safe.

No go, Jez. Time to monkey swing.

I slide across to the other end of the platform and peer through the mesh into the darkness.

Moon's gone and it's badger-hole black out there.

Come on, Star. Bring the big ball back. I need some light here.

I wait.

Slowly, slowly the cloud drape thins and in the dim shine I eye the drainpipe. I reckon it's about a metre away and should take my weight because it's one of those old-fashioned metal types. I'll have to lean right out, get my arms round, then swing my legs across and cling on. Once I stretch out, there's no going back. That's it.

I reach into the darkness and my bones turn to rope.

When I told Star how I edged round the metal cage and how I swung on to the pipe and how it creaked and began to come away from the wall and how the gutter just above my head also started to move, he asked me what would happen if I had fallen. I didn't look down, I said. I told myself not to, and imagined I was just scrambling over the churchyard wall. What stopped the panic and pushed me bit by bit up the pipe, over the swaying gutter and scrambling on to the flat roof above was the thought that I had cheated Big Mother. It was a great feeling. A Good Thing. A Good Thing Big Time.

Once on the roof, it is easy. The skylight hatch is open and the faint smell of the toilets below drifts out into the night air. I hide the can and matches in a section of guttering and return to the hatch. As I slither through the opening, I think: what if Big Mother is waiting below? And I realize I don't care. I've beaten her. I've cheated her. My heart's beating hard in triumph. I've climbed out of trouble. I'm untouchable. I deserve to escape.

I drop on to the floor.

Silence.

A drip pings inside a cistern.

I tiptoe out, then walk down the corridor, all casual. I've done it. I reach my room. I stand in the dark, breathing long and slow.

Safe.

I take off the parka, stick it on the door hook and carefully hide the trainers behind the cupboard. I move towards the bed. Suddenly I'm exhausted. I just want to sleep. I just want blankets wrapping warmth round me.

I'm just about to lift the bedclothes when I stop.

I sniff.

Something isn't right. A strange smell. Pee again? Then I hear sounds. Little squeaks. I look down. In a moment of moonlight I see the bedclothes moving. Are they moving? Is the bed moving? Am I imagining they are squirming?

Freaking hell! I back away. I know what it is.

It's a rat. In my bed. It's Hodge. He's ratted me.

The freaks have got me, again.

I slump to the floor.

The keggin bastard!

6

Bunking Off

I was still shivering.

That's just the fear coming out, said Macker later. Typical Macker. Clever and stupid together.

I must have slept for a bit, right there on the floor. I woke up, stiff, neck aching, wanting to sick up. Why the floor, I was thinking.

I sat up. It was so dark. I checked my watch. It glowed four o'clock.

Across the room, where the bed was, I could hear the faint ticking of my alarm. Through the gap between the curtains I glimpsed a fall of stars. I needed to clear my head so I took a good deep breath . . . and it was then the smell hit me.

Freaking hell! I was wide-awake now.

The rat!

In the bed.

The rat bloated and stinking. I could feel the slow surge of sick coming. I swallowed hard, put my hand over my nose and listened.

There were no sounds from the bed.

Nothing.

Had it got out? I sat very still. Had it eaten its way through the sheets and dragged itself across the floor? Was it lying near me? I backed up against the wall. I got the end of my sleeve and pulled it out till I had enough length to cover my nose and mouth.

I needed to reach the light switch.

I got to my knees, pushed against the wall and slid up till I was standing.

I took a few short side-steps, reached up and flicked the switch.

Click!

Nothing. Crap bulb!

I'd have to try the lamp beside the bed. I edged into the dark of the room, heels raised, toe nudging ahead, one hand over my mouth, the other feeling in front of me. Underfoot, the carpet was smooth and warm. And all the time, I was listening, listening, my ears stretching into the dark.

The alarm was ticking, ticking. The bed was still. Nothing moved.

I was wafting my arm so broadly, scared to miss the lamp, that when I found it I nearly knocked it to the floor. I groped under the shade for the cord, grabbed it and pulled.

Click!

Nothing.

I tried again. Nothing. Was the plug in? Was it turned on? I reached down beside the table, fumbling and swearing. Of course, if I hadn't panicked, if I had taken one moment to think, I would have just pulled up the flex. That would have saved me scrambling around for a manky plug in the middle of the night. That would have told me if it was plugged in or not.

But I didn't do all this. I wasn't thinking. I was cursing Hodge and trying to hold down the puke. I delved into the dark, felt something soft and furry, and screamed.

I staggered back a few steps, and stumbled towards the door. I needed air, fresh, cool air. As I turned and reached for the handle, the door began edging open itself.

'You OK? Jez?'

It was Macker. Thank God. I nodded, then realized it was pit black.

'Yeah,' I whispered hoarsely.

'I knew you'd find it. It was Hodge. Must have closed my window while I was asleep. What you going to do, Jez?'

'Dunno.'

'You better get some air in, this place stinks.'

'I'm not going near that bed.'

'Put the light on.'

'Bulb's gone.'

Macker swore. Then I heard him pull back the curtains. Then I heard him swear again. 'Bastards! They've tied the handles. I'll get my knife.'

He was back in minutes to open the window.

'Here, try this.' He gave me a bulb. While he sorted the window, I got a chair to stand on and reached up to take out the old bulb. It was missing!

Hodge!

I jammed in Macker's bulb, climbed down, groped for the door and hit the switch.

'Rat's over there, Macker. On the floor, by the table with the lamp.' I pointed to the bedside. 'Must have crawled out.'

He walked over, calm as you like, and looked down. Then he bent forward, felt around and lifted something out.

He turned round, and I gawped. Between his finger and thumb he held up a dark, matted, grey shape.

He waved it around.

It was a manky sock!

I shook with laughter. A sock! A manky, poxy sock! I laughed. I laughed till I was fit to puke. I laughed because it was my mate Macker. Because it was us two against the rest. Because I'd burnt Hodge's hut. And because Macker had just hurled the rat-sock out of the window. That got us snorting and giggling again, and we didn't stop till we were lying huddled on the floor, exhausted.

After that, Macker bundled up the sheets, rat and all, and threw them into the corridor. I put on a sweater and he lent me a blanket. As he left my room he said: 'Watch out, Jez. That witch'll have you in the morning.'

Early after breakfast, I was down the Donkey Path, pronto. I told Macker I had to get off 'cos I was down the market picking up another bunch of fireworks to store at Chuffer's.

I stood beside the churchyard wall, looking at the hut. It was a wreck and still smouldering. And the great oak was scorched all down one side. Freaking hell! I could have burnt the lot. Still, I was glad I'd put one over Hodge. He'd be mad. He'd be mental when he found out

65

his stash had gone up in smoke. Tough. He couldn't prove I'd done it. Keep out of his way and I'd be OK.

Then I remembered the rat. No, it wasn't going to be OK. OK was out. Not in a stash of Sundays was it going to be OK. When Hodge had found my bed empty he knew I'd gone on the bunk. Once he'd seen the hut torched, he'd put two and two together. He'd guess it was me, Zippo, burnt his stuff.

I'm going to jam the door tonight. Forget Big Mother.

We're in Dimmo's class, Lab Three, top floor. It's combustion. Macker and I are sitting together and making a list of flammable things. We've got fags, bonfires, petrol, matches, gas, Australian bush fires, rocket fuel, fire bombs. I think of huts and houses. Macker says magnifying glasses and spray cans.

Macker's doing the writing. My swollen fingers make me clumsy with the pencil.

'One day I'll claw her eyes out,' says Macker.

'Ssshhh,' I say. 'She'll hear you.' And I grin, but Macker doesn't see the joke. He's not up for jokes at the moment.

Suddenly, he puts his head in his hands.

I give him a bit of elbow. 'Not here, Mac. Not now.'

He looks up and wipes his eyes with his sleeve. 'I'm going to do a bunk, Jez,' he sniffs. 'I'm doing a goodbye. I've had enough. She's a keggin monster.'

I stare at him. Mac on the bunk! He can't be serious. He wouldn't make the bus queue. They'd have him before he reached the gates even. Then, Macker mate, it'll be the Cupboard, Big Time. A Bad Mother day for you.

'Where'll you go?' I whisper this because I can see Dimmo looking at us over his glasses. 'Write something,' I say. 'Dimmo's on look-out.'

Macker takes the hint.

'Bollocks,' he scrawls right across the page.

'That's my book,' I hiss, and grab a pencil. I use the eraser at the end and start rubbing. I look at Macker. He's grinning. Maybe he is serious.

'When?'

'Tonight.'

Now I know he's crazy.

'I'm going to kill her and the keggin House.'

You're mad, Macker, mad.

Just then Dimmo wakes us all up. He's checking lists. Who's got the most flammable things, he wants to know.

When he comes to us, Macker spouts up. 'Kerosene, methane, naphthalene, dimetrodiahaldehyde.'

Dimmo is gobbed. We all are.

'Dimetri- what, MacNally?'

'DDD for short, sir,' says Macker. 'It's mega combustible, sir. They use it for booster rocket propellant, sir.'

Dimmo frowns and scratches his backside.

'Well, that's very interesting, Mister MacNally,' he says at last. 'Since when have you been studying rocket science?'

'I've read a lot about rockets, sir.' And Macker starts a blather about launches and liquid nitrogen and stuff.

I don't know whether Dimmo's impressed or impatient. I've never heard Macker sound off like this. Even Fat Fat Jane gawps at him. Now she's sure. MacNally is definitely mad. A right head-case. Can't comb his hair, but could put a booster up Dimmo's bum and land him on the moon.

I have a comic-book picture in my head – Dimmo, crash-landed on the lunar surface, his head buried, his legs kicking in the air. In a muffled voice he's shouting: 'Wait till I get out of here, MacNally. I'm going to kill yer.'

Later, at morning break, I'm in the playground keeping an eye out for Hodge when Macker comes up.

'I mean it, Jez. I'm going. Tonight.'

'OK. OK. I believe you.'

'Thing is,' he says, coming closer, 'if I'm going to get to Scotland I need some pounds. I'm skint.'

'Scotland!' I shout this out. Macker gags me with his hand. He looks around as if he expects a full freeze-frame in the playground.

He lets go.

'No one's listening, Mac. It's just you and me.'

He nods, then looks around. Leaning close, he says: 'You won't tell, will yer, Jez mate?'

'Tell what, about Scotland?'

'No. You know, about last night, about me . . . and yer know . . . wetting. Will ya?'

'Course not, mate. I would never.' I'm saying this and thinking, what makes a grown kid like Macker pee in his bed?

'It's only when she comes,' he is whispering. 'I can't help it, honest. It's her makes me. I don't get it, Jez. It just happens. Honest. Honest injun.'

I fist his arm. Give him a bunch. 'She's a witch, Mac. A freaking witch.'

'And there's something else,' he says. 'I need five quid.'

'Five quid! Get a lottery win!'

'Come on, Jez. What about yer fireworks? You've got to have a bit from that.'

'Sshh!' I shrug. 'You're the firework king now,' I say, trying to put him off. 'You're Rocket Man.'

'Yeah, well one day I'll blow it up, the lot. I could do it. I could.'

'Yeah. Yeah. Sure, Mac.'

'Yeah, Walker. Believe it, mate.'

'Blow what up, Mac?'

'The House, what you think.' He pauses. 'If I don't get out,' he says suddenly, 'I'll chop myself.' His voice is quiet. I look in his eyes. They mean what he says.

'Christ, Macker.'

'Come on. You and me are mates. It's only five quid. Just a few rockets and thunderflashes. I can sell them. The snot will buy. I know you've got a stash down at Chuffer's. We'll go fifty-fifty.'

'Ssshh!'

In the end, I agreed. Like he said, we were mates after all, and like me he wanted to get shot of Big Mother and The House and everything. What's more, though he didn't seem to realize it, he could shop me for the torching business. He was the only one who could really prove I was there, propellant in hand, boosting up a bonfire in the graveyard. Poor old Macker. He didn't know it, but I'd have paid to keep him quiet. At the same time, I was willing to help him out.

And anyhow, I always felt the same with Macker, sort of responsible. It was like having a kid follow you around or like having a younger brother, I suppose. If he wasn't around you'd be jumpy in case he'd fallen in the river, and if he was around, he'd be such a freaking pain you'd wish he had fallen in. Macker hadn't a clue, about life and stuff. It's just I'd been there, where it's wild, riding and wrecking, while he, Mad-Mack MacNally, was sat in a book, boosting his sci-fi vocab with words longer than a rush-hour bus queue.

So, we agreed to meet at Chuffer's over lunch break, divide the stash and then he could go down the canal. I'd send regulars like Beef, Ginge, Little Scragg, and some of the snot to meet him. I'd make sure he got a few quids' worth.

Macker grinned and punched my arm.

'Fifty-fifty, Jez. Like real mates.'

I shrugged. Wet-bed Nellie.

'Keep the lot,' I said.

After break, it was History.

Still no sign of Hodge.

I wondered if we'd be working in pairs and if Wilko would talk to me after the row over the drawing. I looked round the classroom. No sign of 'bomber boy' Macker. Every sign of Wilko. She looked right through me as I caught her eye. Blanked me. She had her hair in a ponytail again like girls do. Bad sign? Good sign? I don't know. When a dog's hair rises on its neck you know you're in trouble.

Wilko looks like trouble for me.

Miss C handed out these sheets of paper. One each. They were maps of Appleton Town in the last century, all black and white. You could see the Town Hall and the Infirmary and Saint Bertoline's Church and Lazarus House and the market and the canal. On the screen behind Miss Chips' desk was a map of the town today. We had to work out the main differences. We had to look at the THEN and the NOW. In our books, on a new page, we put three columns. With Miss Chips it's 'new page new work'. It's good to make a fresh start, she'd say. Dimmo's different. So he could save paper, he always makes us follow on from last time's work. He's a miser, like the cooks in The House, they use ice-cream scoops for the mash so no one gets too much.

Miss C tells us to write WHY at the top of the third column. We're to guess why THEN changed to NOW. That's where history happens, she says, in the third column. Facts in the first and second, history in the third.

Somehow I can't concentrate. Hodge and Macker and Wilko are all tumbling about in my mind. Macker especially. I look at Lazarus House on the map. Big Mother's House. The House. Was it always full of lost kids? Full of Mackers? What's changed? Where's the history?

I ask Miss Chips what happened to no-dad kids then. She smiles. She says they went down mines and up chimneys. What happened if you were fat and got stuck up a chimney, said someone. Miss C shook her head. There were no fat kids then. No Fat Fat Janes. You lived thin. You were straw-thin. Waifs you were, says Miss C. Wafer-thins!

Next thing I know, she's looking at my hand. 'What's wrong with your fingers, Jez?'

'Trapped them in a door, miss.'

She takes the other hand. She's got such soft, soft skin. 'All ten?' she says. 'Well, I'm the Queen of Sheba.'

I shrug. 'Who's she, miss?'

'It's not a joking matter, Walker. Is this what you do to each other in that place? They slam doors on you, do they? That's bullying, Jez. It's wrong. I want you to report it to Mrs Dawson. She's the one in charge, isn't she?'

I nod.

'Well, make sure you do or I'll be writing a note to her. It's not on, Jez. Just not on. They look really sore.'

'Yes, miss.'

'Are they?'

'No, miss.'

The bell goes. About time!

I need first lunch so I can get down to Chuffer's and sort out Macker with some bangers and stuff. As I shove books into my desk I become aware of someone standing next to me. I look up.

'Where's my sketch? I want it back.'

Wilko! 'Er . . . I don't have it.'

'You took it.'

'You gave it me.'

'Not to keep. Anyway, you were dead rude about it and I want it back. Now.'

I could see it in my mind's eye, a twist of blackened paper crumbling in the shed flames.

'I need it for Art this afternoon. It's my homework.'

'It's at The House. Soz, I didn't know you needed it.'

'Well, you'll have to get it by the end of break, won't you. It's not far.'

'I can't. I've got something else to do. I can't. I just can't. You'll have to tell Picasso it got lost or something.'

'I spent ages on that, you stupid little prat.'

I stood up. 'Get lost, Wilko. How did I know it was your crappy homework?'

'Quite. Turds know nothing.'

'Slag you.'

Then she smacked me. Dizzied me. A right hefty. I was surprised she had it in her.

She was halfway across the room before I realized what had happened. I started after her, but Fat Fat Jane got in the way. 'Watch it, Walker. Don't mess with girls. You could get roughed up.'

I gobbed her.

Someone grabbed me from behind. It was Miss Chips.

I got detention.

By now I'd missed first sitting, so I decided to give dinner a miss and head for Chuffer's place.

No Macker when I got there. No Chuffer either. It was all locked up. I peered through the window. The old chair was there, the stove, Chuffer's tin mug and, hanging up, his snappin bag and thermos.

I looked round his plot. Mostly weeds and potato plants yellowing. I was about to go when I saw him shuffling along the trampled path through the allotment towards his 'patch'. When he saw me he stopped and began waving a bit of paper. 'Bleedin' Council,' he shouted.

He came up to me, wheezing a bit and red-faced. 'Got me marching orders,' he said. 'Sods want me off me land.' He looked round angrily. 'It's them lot,' he shouted, pointing to a cluster of greenhouses and a huddle of large plastic water-butts. 'Them and their fancy sprinklers and irritation systems and what-have-you. They've complained. They want me off.' He turned to me. 'But, young Jed, the bleeders'll have to carry me off first, I tell yer! Want a cuppa?'

I said I didn't have the time and could I have some of my fireworks and the name was Jez.

He opened the hut door. 'And another thing. I've had some of your lot snooping around.'

'My lot?'

'Kids. Yobs, more like. Bleedin' uniform don't change them. Still yobs.' He took his mug down. 'Here, Jed, fill this. Just take the top. It's sweetest at the top.'

I go out and dip the mug in the water-butt, just scooping from the surface and checking for beetles, drowned flies and moths.

'One of them was a big kid. Sort of slow and daft,' he said as I gave him the mug.

I thought of Spaz.

'And one was nasty and the other a bit mouthy?' I said.

Chuffer nodded. 'Know them?'

'Yeah. Yobs, all of them.'

I watched Chuffer tip the mug water into an old tin pot and place it on a Gaz ring he sometimes used for a quick cuppa.

I had Hodge on my mind. What was he doing down the allotments? Looking for a new place to stash some stuff? Quiet place for a drag?

I looked out of the door. 'Ever thought of growing weed, Chuff?'

'Just take yer gear,' he said. 'What's wrong with good old-fashioned baccy?'

Ten minutes later I was racing down the towpath, looking for Macker and carrying a bag of six rockets. I didn't want him having too many, taking all my profit. A fiver was enough – a fiver for a mate was about right.

No Macker by the bridge, no Macker under the bridge, no Macker on the bridge.

Come on, Mac, where the hell are you?

I checked the concrete stable block next to the lock. It had long been abandoned, but kids went there to smoke stuff and take shots. No Macker though.

Maybe he was in Patel's. That was a corner store, where Nub Lane met Canal Street. It was just up from the lock and Macker and I often called in for smokes or a slice of pizza.

I peered through the window, then pushed my way in. No sign. Patel's was clean out of Mackers.

I wandered back to the towpath.

It was getting late and I was just wondering whether to bunk lessons for the afternoon and join Chuffer again when I saw someone ahead of me on the path. He was coming my way. At first I thought it was Macker. It looked like his lolloping walk.

I stopped and waited for the figure to get a bit closer.

Then I realized.

It wasn't Macker. No way. It was too big, too blobby.

My heart went stop.

It was Spaz.

I turned.

Best to run. But I didn't, not straight away, because there, not fifty metres back up the path, swinging a long white baseball bat, stood Hodge.

7

Mags

No one moved. Canal one side, wall the other. Spaz behind, Hodge ahead.

I was going nowhere. Spaz knew it. Hodge knew it.

So they just watched.

I thought of Star. C'mon, I need you, big black dog. What am I going to do?

'Gotcha now, Walker. We're gonna have you.'

I looked at Spaz. He was grinning. I looked at Hodge. He was licking his tongue in and out, like he was trying to catch the drips off a melting ice-cream.

So, Jez-boy, it's Spaz, cabbage-fist Spaz, or Basher Hodge, the basebat bully.

'What ya got in the bag, Zippo? A rubber dinghy?' Spaz started to laugh and then gobbed into the water. 'Because it's going in the canal,' he spluttered.

'Like you,' shouted Hodge. 'Say 'bye to dry land, Zippo. We're going to put your light out, fireboy.' He raised the bat. 'And then you and I are going to have a little talk.'

Freaking hell!

If the bag was going into the canal I'd rather dump

it myself than let a brickhead like Spaz do it for me.

I was about to pitch it into the water when something gave my brain a good shake and said, no way. It was Star's idea.

Thanks, Star.

I looked up the towpath to where Hodge stood. 'Let me go and you can have these,' I shouted. 'They're worth a bomb.' And I took out a couple of rockets.

'Get stuffed.'

'Let's do him, Hodgy? Let's throw him in the canal.'

I showed another two rockets. 'Look.'

'Rubbish.'

Then I bent down and, before they knew what was going on, I'd jammed two of them in the grass, canalside of the towpath, one pointing in the direction of Hodge, the other pointing at Spaz.

I looked up, whipped out my Zippo and waved it in the air.

Hodge was dead still now. He wasn't swinging his bat. He wasn't kwick-lickin any more. He could see what I was up to.

'Take a step, one step, and whoosh, I light these,' I shouted, looking first at Hodge then Spaz.

Neither of them moved.

The big cones of the rockets nosed out of the tall grass, like red torpedoes. Only then did I catch a glimpse of the name on the side of the rocket. *StarBuster* it said.

Good one, big dog!

I grabbed a couple of small rockets from the bag. One I jammed in my belt, the other I held in my left hand, aiming it directly at Hodge's head. Under its blue touch-paper I now held the Zippo, ready to flick on the flame.

'Any nearer, Hodgy, and I light this one, then the big ones.'

'Right little terrorist, aren't we.'

Neither of them moved. The three of us stood there – Spaz frowning, Hodge folding his arms, me standing sideways, facing the canal and checking them both, left and right, cocking my head first at one then at the other, like a puppet on strings.

They stood still. Not hesitating, just waiting.

The water lap-lapped, traffic hummed in the distance, and far, far above us, almost sound-proofed by the clouds, an invisible plane droned on.

Then it began to rain.

Rain! Freaking rain!

I kicked the bag into the canal. It slid under the water, like the torso of some animal, a dog drowning or a giant rat.

I could see Hodge had worked it out.

'It's raining, Jez boy. Better keep yer fire dry. Zippo don't like the wet, does he? 'Cos we can wait all day waiting for the rain.' And he started swinging the bat round his head.

I looked up at the sky. Darker clouds were gathering.

I needed to move before everything got soaked. Hodge meant it. He'd wait all day, swinging his freaking big white bat.

No choice.

I looked down the towpath at Spaz. He had that dead-brain grin all over him, the dimbo.

It needed wiping off his face.

He needed a *StarBuster* up his backside.

In one movement I flicked on Zippo, bent down and put the flame to the touch-paper. It crackled and sparkled red.

StarBuster go!!

Now Hodge was shouting: 'Look out, Spaz. Drop. Get on yer face, yer dummy.'

Your turn, Hodgy-boy. Another match and the second rocket was crackling.

Whoosh!

The Spaz rocket arrowed away and immediately veered off over the canal. I didn't wait for the crash and I didn't check on Hodge. I was off, charging towards Spaz, who was still lying face down on the towpath. I could hear Hodge shrieking something and I could see Spaz lift his head as I raced nearer.

Suddenly he was on his feet with his arms stretched across the width of the towpath. I slithered to a halt, hardly three metres from him. He was grinning again. I lifted the Zippo and lit the rocket in my hand.

Horror stiffened his face.

'Get out of the way,' yelled Hodge from behind.

I jabbed the rocket at Spaz. Suddenly a spew of sparks shot up my sleeve and it flashed from my grip. With a whooping cry, I ran forward, like I was Robocop or the Terminator juiced up and about to blow.

Spaz threw himself to one side, slipped and tumbled backwards into the canal, arms and legs splayed out, like he was falling on to a soft bed. The rocket veered after him, shot through the splash and buried itself in a clump of brambles on the far side of the canal.

And I, I ran. I ran as hard and as fast as I'd ever run in my life. Along that towpath towards the lower locks.

I knew I had a head start on Hodge. But, so what. Hodge was big and fast and he had a baseball bat hard enough to bruise your brains.

I never looked behind. Not once. Right up to the bridge. You win if you don't look behind.

I reached the locks and slithered down the cobbled steps beside one of the big wooden arms. I dashed under the bridge and skidded on to the towpath again.

I knew he'd be closing in. I knew he could brain me. It wouldn't take long. To catch me. He could be there, now, right behind me, about to strike, the bat raised high, ready to crash down.

I had to check, had to check.

I turned. Looked over my shoulder. Just a quick glance. Nothing more.

I never saw the mooring rope.

I crashed to the ground, right shoulder thudding into the gravel.

I staggered up, dizzy and wobble-kneed. Someone was grabbing me. 'What's up, Walker?'

Freaking hell!

Wilko!

'It's Hodge,' I said hoarsely. 'He's after . . .'

Before I could finish, she was dragging me towards the barge moored by the towpath.

'In here, quick.'

I tumbled over the side and scrambled through a small swinging door.

'Get down. Don't move,' she hissed, landing next to me. We were both lying on the floor, me heaving, she scanning the window, eyes moving left and right.

I held my breath. Someone pounded past. Then it went silent. Only the croaking of water at the side of the barge interrupting.

'He's gone,' she whispered. Her face was close to mine and I could smell that posh soap again. 'Stay there.'

Slowly she got up and, one by one, began to close the curtains on the towpath side. When she'd finished, she clambered over me, pulled the cabin doors shut and shot the bolt home.

I struggled to my feet.

'Are you all right?'

'Shoulder's killing.'

'You've got blood there.' She pointed to my arm. The sleeve was pushed up to the elbow and the skin was clawed red.

'Hodge!'

'What happened?'

I sat down and began to explain.

'Keep your voice down. He might come back.'

I told her about the porridge and the ratting. I told her about The House and Macker and Big Mother and how snots got wasped and stuff. I don't know why I told her all this. I hardly knew her. Anyway, it all came out.

I didn't tell about Star. She wouldn't believe it. Talking to a dog? She'd think I was a right saddo. 'Wise up,' she'd say. Best keep it between me and Star, just the two of us. If everyone knew, it wouldn't be special. Yeah, words'd put him in a cage, tie him down. Everyone could see him, like he was in a zoo or something. But no one owns him. Not Star. Not even me. He just lets me stroke him sometimes. Talk in his ear.

Thing is, Star is invisible really. Only I can see him – when he lets me. Most of the time he's invisible. If I told Wilko, she'd see him too and Star might get mad. He might disappear forever.

I didn't tell her about burning the hut either. She wouldn't like that. I'd get an earful if she knew. Or she'd tell Miss Chips. Girls are like that. You can't always trust them.

She goes quiet for a bit and then she wants to know why whoever runs the place doesn't do something about people like Hodge. I say the big question is, why who- ever runs the country doesn't do something about people like Big Mother and all the other Big Mothers out there. Macker said this once to me. He wanted to burn her, but I said that you need Big Mothers to keep all the Hodges in place. I thought that was quite a clever thing to say.

Mags gives me a funny look. 'If we got rid of the Hodges, and the Spazs and all the Maggots we wouldn't have to bother about the Big Mothers,' she says.

I shrug because I want it to look as though I'm think- ing about what Mags has just said. In truth, I don't quite get what she's on about. Then I remember what Miss

Chips said about Mags seeing things differently. Maybe this is it. She just sees things I don't. Maybe I see things differently too, things she doesn't. Trouble is, if we all see differently, how do we get to see eye to eye about anything?

'Well!' I say after a pause, 'You haven't met Big Mother. She's a witch. Big Witch.'

Then she surprises me.

'Yes, I have. I've been to the home,' she says. 'And met Mrs Big Mother Dawson. Yesterday.'

'Yesterday? You went to The House and met Big Mother? That witch! Why?'

'Ask if I could look round the building.'

'Why?'

'For the History project, stupid.'

'I thought we were doing the church.'

Mags shakes her head. 'Changed my mind.'

'What about *my* mind? Suppose I don't want to do The House?'

Mags shrugs.

Tough. She's made her mind up.

'But it wasn't on the list Miss Chips gave us.'

'So? We'll get extra marks for showing initiative. Anyway, Fat Fat Jane's decided she's doing the church. I'm not sharing. She'll be forever nicking stuff off us.'

I say nothing. I'm not sure I want Mags digging up the mank on Lazarus House. Telling her about it is one thing, having her coming in and turning it over is another. After all it's my mank we're talking about here. And once Mags starts sniffing about, she's bound to see I don't smell all roses. I'd feel like a pig caught with his feet in the trough. I don't want her to see me like that.

No way.

'You can't trust Big Mother,' I say. 'Next time she'll throw you out.'

Mags shakes her head. 'No she won't. In fact, she's already invited me back – to the bonfire party next week.'

I gawp. 'You're having me on.'

Wilko shakes her head.

'But why? She hates interferers. She's a witch, I tell you.'

'She was OK to me.'

'Well, she's not OK to me. She wallops you for nothing at all.'

Wilko is silent for a bit. 'Everyone seems to have it in for you – Hodge, Big Mother, Fat Fat Jane. Why's that?'

I shrug. 'Dunno.'

'And I've just saved you from another good doing-over. Hodge'd have thrown you in the canal.'

'Yes. Thanks.'

'And you owe me an apology.'

'Yeah.'

'Well, let me hear it. Tell me I'm not a slag like you said.'

'You're not a slag like I said. Now, tell me I'm not a turd.'

'You're not a turd. Now say sorry for the slag thing, and then we're equal.'

'No we're not. You clouted me as well.'

'You deserved it. Now, say sorry. Go on. Actual sorry.'

'I have, just.'

'No. I mean a real sorry.'

I stare at her.

They want everything, girls. They want you to grovel.

'What for?'

''Cos I want you to.'

'You're just rubbing my nose in it. You want me to crawl, just because you saved me from a clobbering.'

She looks hard at me. 'Well, so you're not big enough to apologize. Tough boy Walker, frightened of saying sorry.'

'Hey, what is this?' My voice rises.

'Watch it, Walker; Hodge'll hear you.'

'I've said as much sorry as I'm going to,' I whisper fiercely. 'Apologies are for puftas, blouses, snots.'

Wilko stands up and starts to walk towards the door. She begins to unbolt it.

'What's up?' I say uneasily. 'What you doing?'

'I just thought I'd go outside and see if that mental case is still around.'

'You're the mental case, Wilko. If he sees you, he'll know I'm here.'

'I know.'

I look at her. I can't believe it. She's going to shop me. Do a snot on me.

She folds her arms. 'So, apology or Hodge, which is it?'

She has me. We both know it.

'Well? I'm not waiting all day.'

'Sorry,' I mumble.

'Louder.'

'I'm freaking sorry,' I shout. 'Soz. Soz. Soz. That do ya?'

Suddenly we freeze. Someone's outside.

'Anyone there?' says a voice.

'Hodge.' I mouth the word to Wilko. She puts a finger to her lips and looks at me fiercely. Come off it, Wilko. What you think I'm going to do? Invite Hodge in for a Coke and a plateful of Wagon Wheels?

She turns round and begins very carefully sliding back the bolt to lock the cabin door once again.

I don't dare move more than a blink. Did he hear me shout? Did he?

We wait. Nothing. He's gone, hasn't he?

I watch Wilko looking anxiously at the window. Can he see through? Are the curtains fully closed? I sink my head down so my cheek is resting on the cold plasticky floor. It smells of disinfectant. Dead near my face I can see a single baked bean, furred with mould, trapped under a locker drawer.

Suddenly there's a bang at one of the windows just above me. Then another and another. Wilko's face is wide with alarm.

'It's him,' I say. 'He's smashing the window.'

'Right,' she hisses. She jumps up and, slamming back the bolt, wrenches open the doors and runs out.

'Don't,' I shout. 'He'll kill yer.'

But she's gone.

I run after, clamber on to the towpath and stop dead. There is Hodge, bat raised ready to clobber the window again, and there is Wilko, heavey-breathey now, stone in hand, ready to clobber Hodge.

When he sees me, he lowers the bat. 'Oooh. What have we got here, a little love nest? Ahhh,' he sneers.

'Shut your big gob,' says Wilko.

I shiver inside. Hodge'll do her for that.

'Watch yours, yer little tart, or you'll get a face full of this.' And he waves the bat at her. Then suddenly he grins. 'Wilko and Zippo Walker with his wicked wick. Bunking on the barge. Naughty. Naughty. Naughty. Wait till they hear about this. What will little Miss Chips say?'

'Get lost, Hodge,' I say.

'We're working on a project, so get stuffed,' says Wilko.

I groan inside. Swallow that, Hodge. Some hope! Girls!

Just then a man and his dog appear, walking towards us down the towpath. Wilko waves to him. Hodge takes one look and starts to move away from the barge. Suddenly he begins to run and as he passes me he shoves out his arm and rams my wrecked shoulder. I jerk backwards with the sudden pain, slip and slither down the bank till I'm standing, waist deep, in the canal.

Wilko stands above me, shaking her head.

'It's not my fault. He shoved me. Give us a hand, Wilko.'

'The name's Mags,' she says.

'Mags. Wilko. What difference does it make? Give us a hand, would yer.'

'It makes a lot of difference. "Mags" means I help you. "Wilko" means you get out yourself.'

I'm getting dead cold now, so I grab a handful of grass and start to haul myself on to the bank.

I don't know if it is the cold or the pain in my shoulder, but I find I just haven't got the strength, and I slip back.

Wilko reaches down a hand. I make a grab for it and she moves it away.

'Hey, look, ducks,' she says.

'OK. OK. What's your problem? You want to play silly sods. Get me out of here.'

I pause.

'Mags,' I add between chattering teeth.

'That's the magic word,' she says and, taking hold of my wrist, she pulls me up shivering.

She persuades me to let her mum 'sort me out'. Normally I wouldn't be seen dead going down the posh end of town, and never, not never, with a girl. But I'm so cold by now that the idea of a hot shower and a decent tea sounds dead good. I'll go. Just this once, though. Anyway, I don't want to meet Hodge and I don't want Big Mother finding me soaked to the skin in the middle of the afternoon. She'd go mental. 'Filthy rat,' she'd say. 'Filthy little rat.'

Wilko steps back into the barge and begins padlocking the cabin doors. It's only then I catch on.

'How come you've got a key? Is it yours? You own a barge?'

'Sort of. Was my dad's. He's left it. Now it's my mum's, but she hates it. She's an earth one, not a water one.'

'Earthworm?'

'Earth person, cloth ears. Some of us are water, some are air, some are fire.'

Sounds bonkers to me. Not that I care much just at the moment. All I know is, I'm standing on the towpath, very much a water person, and what I really want to be is a fire person, dry and warm.

'Let's go,' I say. 'I'm f-f-freezing.'

8

Pink Rabbits

We stopped at Mags' front gate. Leading up to the front door was a narrow, paved path, squeezed thin where it ran between two huge holly bushes. The house was dark, and because the shrubbery kept the streetlight at a dim distance I'd no idea how big it was.

You could hear the water dripping from gutters and tick-ticking on to the paving like a run-down clock. I tried to breathe dead shallow because the smell of the earth, all mould and wet leaves, hung in your face like bad breath. It reminded me of the churchyard and graves heaving open and dark things coming forth.

Mags opened the door.

'Mum's out,' she said. 'But she'll be back soon. Now you'll have to wait.' She pulled the freebie newspaper out of the letterbox and made me stand on it so I wouldn't drip on the wooden floor.

I looked around. Books were piled on each one of the stairs and ran all the way up to the top like another set of steps. On one side of the hall stood a table, crowded with half-finished candles in bowls and brass holders and old wine bottles.

Mags, who'd seen me staring, said they were good for meditation. Candlelight was gentle; it kept the everyday world in the dark and focused the mind on the spirit-flame. The real world was the spirit world. The flame was a sign of its presence. That's what her mum told her anyway. The world is full of invisible beings.

I said we'd had supper once with candles, when the electric went at The House, but we didn't get any spirits turning up.

Mags said it wasn't funny. Places had to be, first and foremost, spirit-friendly. 'No spirit would be seen dead in a place like that House,' she added.

Opposite the table, hanging by chains, was a huge mirror. The frame was blue and fringed with feathers sticking out from behind the top and the sides. Beneath it stood a statue of a woman holding a torch, like they have at the Olympics, with the flame bit made of white glass. Mags said there was a bulb inside and showed me how it lit up when you pressed a switch behind the head. I could see at least three dead moths inside. It reminded me of Chuffer's place, where insect husks litter the windowsills draped in dusty webs.

Just then, Mags' mum arrived. She gave Mags a hug and called her sweetheart.

No hugs for me thank you, mama Wilko. Hugs is not on my menu.

'Well, Jez,' she smiled after Mags had introduced me. 'First stop, the shower. Come on, you stink. You look like a drowned rat. And let's have those shoes.'

I was bustled upstairs, shown into the bathroom and told to throw out my wet clothes.

But first, she tossed me a towel. It was a fancy purply colour and smelled like the beach and the sea.

'Use this when you've finished, Jez.' She handed me a pink coat thing. 'It's Mags'.'

'That's OK,' I said. 'I don't mind.'

She closed the door and I stood there like a prat, holding up this long fluffy coat covered in girl smell and with a large toothy rabbit printed on the back.

Pink rabbits! If Hodge could see me now.

I sit on the edge of the bath and look around. The whole room is tiled, floor to ceiling, in pale green, and they've got a shiny chrome bowl full of posh-smelling leaves and things and a tall vase in one corner sprouting a bundle of sticks. What are they doing in a bathroom? Maybe they burn them for the smell, like in temples and things.

At the end of the bath is the shower cubicle. In The House, it's crap because the showers get blocked up and cold, scummy water runs all over the place. I like baths the best, but we only get one a week usually and it's only good if you get in early before all the hot goes. But it can be a Bad Thing when Big Mother comes. She can turn a Good Thing into a Bad Thing anytime she tries. Sometimes she makes you have a cold bath. She says it's to show us we're lucky having The House, and to remind us that, when we grow up, life outside won't be so easy. It's to harden us up, she says. She filled mine almost to the top once, filled it with icy cold, and then she made me take off all my clothes, there and then, right in front of her. I could hardly breathe, it was so cold. She made me lie back so only my face was out. I tried to get up, but she pushed me down, right under with the Hand. I nearly drowned and when I got out she had the towel and started drying me all over with her good hand, squeezing and rubbing till it hurt and I was sore.

I get up and open the shower door and fiddle with the controls. I turn to check on the towel and see I've left a dark bum-print on the edge of the bath. I grab some bog roll and wipe it clean.

I step into the shower. At The House, they're never warm, never tingling and spurting hot. More squirts than showers.

I read the words round the control dial. I turn it to 'massage' and water pulses out dead fast and splatters me.

I close the door and stand under the pelleting water. Squirls of mud dissolve in the sluicing water and spiral down the plughole. I turn the controls to pulse and water smacks me in the face, hard spray blasting away the smell of canals and rats and cold rain. It's washing Hodge out of my hair and Big Mother and The House. It's washing away the stink of bedwet and Spaz gob and the cold slime of upped porridge. I run the silky water over me, palms slipping down my belly, along my thighs, over my arms. I'm glistening, I'm clean, I'm steamed warm.

On the misted glass of the cubicle door, I write 'JEZ' with my finger and imagine that the light in the ceiling, shining through the hot fogginess, is one of the landing lights of a flying saucer coming to collect me, a small earthling, and take me back to planet Zeros. On planet

Zeros, the weather is always mild and warm. It's what we call a temperate climate. Miss Chips likes a temperate climate. She'd like Zeros. You can swim in the rivers any time of the year. They're all warm. There's no seasonal variation. It's like swimming in Greece or down south. Zeros has six suns so that, when one disappears, there's always another to take its place, and it's never hot enough for sunburn.

I find my way down to the kitchen, where I can hear the two of them talking. The door's half open and I hesitate before entering.

'He tries to be hard,' Mags is saying, 'because you have to be in that home place. I don't think he's really hard. I think it's all he knows. It's not fair. The big kids beat up the little kids. It's just not fair.'

I hear a few pans rattle.

'The system beats them all up,' says Mags' mum. 'By the time they get to your age, sweetheart, they are so bruised, they shout with pain all the time.'

Then silence. I guess Mags is trying to work out what her mum meant. So am I. Bruised? Not me, mate.

Then I hear her say that I'd called her a slag.

I groan.

Slag!

It sounds like filth. It feels like mud in yer mouth. I run my fingers down the pink silky edging of the Mags' coat.

'And what did you call him?' I hear her mother ask.

'Nothing much. But he apologized after. I made him.'

'You made him?'

'Yeah.'

'That's hard. That is hard.'

'It's for his own good. You don't talk to girls like that.'

'No.'

'And he keeps calling me Wilko, so I made him stay in the canal till he called me Mags.'

'In the canal? That was very hard on him. Wasn't it, sweetheart? He's only a kid, as you say. No mum. No dad.'

Mags says nothing. Then: 'I didn't make him go in the canal. Someone pushed him. Anyway, he's got a dad, in Australia.'

'Australia? That's a big place.'

A Big Place it is. Suddenly, I'm thinking of Macker. Macker used to talk of the Big Places. Out There are the Big Places, he'd say. That's where he wanted to be, in the Big Places. Out There in the desert or Africa or the Atlantic Ocean. Out There, by himself. Stuff Chuffer's Hut and the canal and the Donkey Path and the Odeon. Macker wanted a Big Place all for himself. Poor Macker. He's a headcase.

'Not having a mum is what I call hard, Mags.'

Silence. Then a clatter of knives or plates or something.

'We all have a mum side and a dad side,' Mags' mum was saying. 'Inside us. Heart and head.'

Silence.

I could see now where Mags got some of her funny ideas. A mum side? Didn't make sense to me. Anyway,

I hadn't got time for hearts. I was thinking about stomachs and about how empty mine was. I was starving.

I looked across the hall and saw myself in the mirror – a hungry kid with spiky wet hair, thin face and dressed in a pink rabbit bathrobe. Hard Jez, bunny boy. I stepped into the kitchen and the smell of meat pie, and I decided, there and then, that Mags' mum was OK.

When she saw me, she came over, ruffled my hair, said it needed more drying and gave me another towel.

'Sit down, Jez. You're all skin and grief. I'm going to feed you up. I've rung the home. Told them you're out to tea. I must say the woman sounded . . .' she paused.

'Mad?' I said.

'Cold. Frosty.'

She checked my hair again. She had soft hands and smelt sort of spicy. She always seemed to be smiling without actually smiling. She was a sweet earth one and had none of the sour breath of the wet soil outside. None of the mank of the canal. And though she did treat me like I was Mags' little brother, it was a good feeling to have someone sorting you out.

She gave me a lift back to The House. What did my dad do in Australia, she wanted to know. I said he was a gold digger. He panned for gold, and when he had made his fortune, he was coming back home. It was just a matter of time. After that, she asked no more questions. I don't think she believed me.

When we got to The House, she said she'd come in and see I was all right. I think Mags had told her about some of the things that went on there, like Hodge and ratting and about the porridge. But I said I was OK. Once you start making trouble, trouble won't leave. Big Mother didn't like outside people. She didn't like the SS, doctors or anything. Interferers, she called them. Nobody interferes in this House, she said one breakfast time. This is our House. We are all one family. We don't talk to interferers. Nobody talks to interferers. Remember that. Nobody. Interferers ask questions. Poke their noses in where they're not wanted. Remember – no answers. There are to be no answers.

I hurried up the steps to the front door. She was waiting. Called me into her office. Wanted to know where I'd been. Who was the woman? Who did she think she was! What did she want? What did I tell her?

I just shrugged. I knew Big Mother didn't like that. 'Come on, out with it. Something's been going on. What?'

'Nothing,' I said. She began to move the Hand from behind her back. 'I said we were all one big family,' I added quickly. 'That's all.'

'Yes, Walker, and don't you ever forget that.'

Big Mother stares at me for some time. Big Mother has a podgy face and her skin looks like the skin of a puffball. She is sitting behind her desk, and from where I'm standing I can see patches of pink scalp through her thin grey hair. Baby mice pink. I notice these things because I don't want to look her in the eyes. But it's no good. It never is. After a bit, they seem to get right inside your head, whether you look or not. It's like God knows what you are thinking, deep down. Big Mother does, too. She waits and then she pounces and you're under her claws.

'Well?' she says at last. 'What else have you got to tell me?'

I say nothing. What else is there?

'You know, Walker.'

I've no idea. Is she having me on or what?

'You don't know,' she mimics me. 'I've had the police here today. Interfering. Asking questions. About you. About The House. Questioning me. Me! As if it was all my fault. Poking their noses in. All because of you. You're going to get us a bad name. You're letting us down. Letting us all down. Out there they soon hear about us. About The House. They look for trouble out there. And you give it to them, hand it out on a plate. They say we're full of criminals. The House is full of Bad uns. The police come round. What do you expect them to think?'

'Who?' I say, dead confused.

'People,' says Big Mother, leaning towards me so I can see the pink patches on her scalp. It's like an atlas with countries blotched on her skin. I think of Macker. Australia is Out There slap on the back of her head.

'You're a Bad un, Walker. You're bringing this House down. And I'm not going to have it, do you hear?'

I nod. And all the time I'm thinking about the police. Is it the hut and the burning? Must be.

She'll kill me if she finds out.

'You're our bad apple, Walker. But you're going to mend your ways. You're going to learn to co-operate.

From now on you're under curfew. No going out after school. No going to tea with lah-di-dah ladies. You stick to your own kind from now on. And so you don't get bored, you can start with a bit of polishing. That'll teach you. And you can start now. You've got an hour before supper. Do the first stairs. You know where the cleaners' cupboard is. Now, out! I'll be round to check you later. And get a real polish. I want those stairs shining. Shining. I want to see your nasty little face in them.'

I'm kneeling halfway up the first stairs. Every now and again, a kid goes past. No one says anything. If you're caught talking to someone on routine, you get the same and sometimes double. On routine you're on your own.

The worst bit is the smell. It won't go away. It's just there all the time, the smell of the polish. It's The House B.O. Everyone catches it. You can always tell a kid from here, 'cos he smells of it. That's what they say: people, teachers. House kids smell. They think you never wash. They don't understand. It gets in your skin, your hair and your clothes. And if she's had you on polishing, you can smell it on your fingers at night in bed. It's like thick tomato ketchup and comes in wacking big tins and you have to scoop it out and smear it on your cloth with a flat bit of wood like a ruler.

I hate polishing. It kills your knees. And it gets in your eyes. Macker says it's because of the paraffin. And it gets in your mouth, and if you do it before supper, like a whole landing, then all the food tastes of polish after and you just want to spit it out.

Skirting's the worst, 'cos if you get the red on the wall,

she goes mental and it kills your back and your knees. Stairs are best 'cos you don't bend so much and you only have to do the step, not the up as well.

I'm looking at my hands. We're supposed to wear gloves, but I couldn't find any in the cupboard. We're not supposed to do it without gloves. Try telling that to Big Mother. She'd skin you.

I can just see my face in the shine. A shadow face. Me, trapped. Am I rubbing myself out or polishing myself up? I sit up and stretch my back. I feel hungry. It's suppertime. I'm going to miss supper.

One day, I'll be out of here. One day.

Suddenly a hand is gripping my neck and forcing my head down. 'Take a good look, Walker. Is it shiny? Can you see your face?'

I can't possibly. She has my forehead flat on the wood. She is leaning on me, pressing me down. I breathe in the invisible mank of her, the damp, rubbery whiff of her, and taste the slow odour of paraffin.

'It's right under your nose, boy. Can't see for looking? Better try harder.' She relaxes her grip and slowly I sit up again. 'Oh, go to supper,' she says, suddenly irritated. 'Get out of my sight.'

Later, I'm talking to Star. I show him my red hands. He says soon it will be time to take revenge. He won't tell me what he's planning.

I smile. Watch out, Big Mother, Star's coming.

I tell him about Mags and her mum and about Hodge, and I say what a great idea of his about the rockets. We laugh about Spaz falling in the canal. And I finish by asking Star to find my dad in Australia and say I'm asking about him and when is he coming home. If Star can't find him, no one can. And if Star doesn't find him, then that's it. He's gone. Lost.

It'll just be me and Star forever.

9

Luscious Green

Next day, early morning, I'm in the lavs. The rain is pelleting against the skylight and I'm scrubbing my fingers, one by one, trying to get rid of the red.

Macker's beside me, sniffing and yawning. I look around. No Maggot. No Hodge.

'Where'd you go? Yesterday?' I said. 'I was down the canal. No you. No fireworks.'

Macker shrugged.

I tell him about Spaz and Hodge and the rockets. I leave out the bit about the barge and Mags. Well, he might get the wrong idea.

'Soz, Jez. Picasso had me on detention.'

'What for?'

'Lost me Art homework.'

We'd been doing perspective. We had to draw a box and work out the vanishing point. According to Picasso, our Art teacher, things disappear into the distance. Sort of shrink to a speck. Then to nothing.

Everything has a vanishing point. Like me and you and Big Mother. And Macker's homework. That's always disappearing.

Macker and me are going to find out Big Mother's vanishing point. Get her in perspective. Disappear her. Vanish her off the face of the earth.

So we said. But it's going to take more than a bit of drawing to cut Big Mother down to size.

At breakfast, no Big M, no hand inspection. Beans and fried tomatoes and sausages. Hodge slapping it on. Not for me. He stirs and stirs and then blobs my plate with some bean goo about the size of a baby mouse.

'Soz, Walker. All that's left.'

Keggin liar!

He forks out two sausages. Freaking midgets! Close to vanishing point. One more minute in the pan and they'd disappear in their own sizzle.

Rest of the day turned out Bad Day Big Time. Especially for Macker.

It was OK till Art, last two lessons of the afternoon. No perspective today. Perspective put on hold. Parents' Evening was coming up and Chadders, our headmaster, wanted something bright for the entrance hall.

Macker wanted to paint exploding fireworks. Picasso told him we were doing tie-and-dye. Hodge said T&D was right girlie, but he did it anyway because he was good at art. Picasso lets him run the place, dishing out paints and paper with one hand and nicking new brushes with the other. He flogs these to some guy on the market or to Patel's.

I suppose T&D is a bit posher than slopping paint on

sugar paper, a bit more arty, bit more what parents like. I suddenly think of my dad. He'd like bright, light things because that's how it is in Australia: blue skies, polish-red rocks, glittery lizard skin. He'd look at my T&D, crinkly with green and yellow stars, and say: 'Good one, son. Good on yer,' like they do in *Neighbours*.

Then he vanishes out of sight and I know he won't be there. Cast-off kids don't have parents. And Miss Chips won't be able to tell him about the History project or anything.

Then – a right disaster! Macker is moving a tray of green dye between tables. Why? 'Cos he's Macker and that's what he does. Whenever he's around, things wobble. They back off. Don't feel safe. So they panic and fall and break and tear and stumble and crash.

I watch as he moves a wobbling plastic tray. It's full of green dye. 'Luscious Green'. That's what it says on the bottle. I follow him. I know what's going to happen, what always happens. He catches the edge of the tray on the corner of the table and spills the lot. It splashes all over Fat Fat's shoes and white socks. She leaps up, splashes Mac with some colourful words of her own and storms out of the room.

Macker is not just splashed, he's soaked. His hands and trousers are Luscious Green.

Martian Macker leaves for the Boys' lavs, and in the chaos of the clean-up I sneak out to help him.

'Freaking hell, Macker! Come on! Picasso's having a fit.'

He looks up.

105

'Picasso's OK. But what about Big Mother? She'll go mental.'

And she did.

It happened like this.

I walk home with Macker and Mags joins us, which is OK 'cos Macker is there. She wants to know what it is with us two. Why Mac's got green hands and I've got red ones. Is it body art or what? She's read about body painting in some poncy art book. No, Mags, body art it's not.

The skin is just another canvas to paint on, she says. It's a way of expressing yourself. Australian aborigines do it. Tattoos are the same thing. Skin doodling.

I'm thinking of Big Mother and wondering how she's going to express herself when she sees Macker's hand-painting job. It won't be the kind of skin treatment girlies like Wilko dream about.

Macker frowns. He's not really used to Mags. But in some ways she's as daft as he is. Just 'cos you put on lipstick and that blusher stuff doesn't mean you're Van Goff. That's not art, that's make-up, Mags. Got it?

Teatime. We grab slices of bread and sit down. It's gloopy stew. No Big Mother. Gloop's hot and salty and makes a freaking great gravy sandwich.

I'm just wiping the plate dead clean, when everything goes quieter. I don't need to check. Big Mother's back.

I see Mac slip his hands under the table out of sight. He waits. Finish yer gloop, Mac, or she'll notice and want to know what's wrong with the good clean food she provides and why you aren't eating it. Come on, Mac, come on.

Mac doesn't move.

I decide to switch my finished plate for his.

Just as I grab it, she turns.

'Walker!'

She storms over.

She turns on Macker.

'Eyes too big for your stomach, MacNally?' she says, standing behind him.

Macker doesn't move. He just sits there like a frog, hunched over, head sunk in his shoulders.

'Sit up, boy. Been eating sweet rubbish again, so you can't benefit from the good wholesome food we put in front of you? No wonder you're a pasty-faced apology for a boy.'

Macker shifts slightly.

Hold it, Macker. Don't let her get to you.

'Finish it,' she orders.

Slowly, slowly, Mac drags one hand into the open and reaches for a fork.

At first, she doesn't notice his fingers are frog green.

Macker takes a mouthful.

Then she explodes. Grabs his coat at the shoulder and heaves him up.

Macker splutters brown gloop down his chin.

She's shivering with anger. What's he done? What's this? She holds his hand at arm's length, like it's some bit of mank. What does he think he's playing at?

107

'It wasn't my fault, Mrs Dawson, honest and hope to die,' says Macker. He talks dead quick and is shaking his head. 'It just spilt, in Art. It's Luscious Green.'

'Luscious Green? Just spilt?' sneers Big Mother. 'I'll give you Luscious Green.'

This is a Black Book offence, Mac. This is Black Book Big Time, mate.

No one breathes. Not a spoon or fork or knife clinks.

Everyone waits.

Then she sees the trousers.

'You little vermin!' She looks like she's shouting. Her mouth is wide open, but she's too mad to get the full shout out, and it sounds like a rat is squealing from her throat.

'Get them off. Now. This minute.'

Macker just stands there, like he's paralysed. Get his trousers off! She can't be serious.

She grabs his belt, tears at the buckle and rips it off. She steps back. Jabs her finger at the floor.

Macker unzips and slowly lets the trousers fall round his ankles.

She holds out her hand. Macker steps out of the trousers, picks them up and hands them to her. She holds them at arm's length.

I watch his fingers trying to edge his shirt-tail over his bum and his greenish knicks.

'You disgusting little animal! Look at you.'
The dye has soaked through the trousers and his legs are printed and patched with green. Frog-legs Macker. The witch! Double Black Booking Mac.
Whole chapter, the full works.

'Rest of the meal, in the corner,' says Big Mother between tight teeth. She gives the trousers to one of the snots and tells him to put them in the laundry.

Macker slowly walks between the tables, past the backs of silent kids, past the hatches and into the corner by the cutlery table.

We all watch him. As he bends his head, I see his shoulder give a slight shiver. Hold it, Mac. Hold it.

Big Mother turns to the rest of us. She points to Macker. 'That's what comes of being thoughtless and stupid. Let that be an example to you all. No one's born filthy, they get that way by laziness and being idle-minded. You've got to take pride in yourselves so you can bring pride to The House. Not shame, like him over there. This is a good House. What are they going to think, people out there, when they see this sort of thing? I'll tell you. They'll think we've got second-hand kids here and no better. I'm not having that. You may have started bad apples, but you're not going to go out of here bad apples.'

She stopped. Pointed to me. I stood up before I knew what I was doing. 'Go and get MacNally a pair of shorts. You know where from?'

I nodded. I knew all right – the Tide-over cupboard. Where all the mank from older kids was stored, to be handed on to any snot who lost their decent stuff or wore it out too soon. You got old sweaters, shirts, games stuff, even trainers in the Tide-over. No one liked getting Tide-over gear. You had to put it on there and then. No washing out someone else's dirt. All you could do was hold your nose and try shaking out the old stink, it was that bad.

Shorts for Macker, again! He'd die.

As I climbed up to the first floor, I was thinking that at least Macker didn't blub this time. Maybe he was toughening up. He probably would later, blub I mean, in bed. But then, maybe not. Somehow, Big Mother's spit and blather hadn't seemed to crush him like before times.

I wouldn't blame him. Blubbing's allowed. Star says blubbing's allowed. On your own, of course. Not when anyone's around. I mean, that's just a way of getting attention, like waving a flag or something. Blub washes away some of the mank in your life. Like swilling muck off yer plate. Girls blub a lot. But that's different. They can't help it. I think they enjoy it. It's in their nature. I've even seen girls blubbing together, holding hands and

110

blubbing over something or nothing, right there, in front of everyone. Honest. No lie.

You don't see adults cry. That's because they begin to dry up once they get to teen time. OK, you see them in films and things, at funerals and disasters, but not in real life, real real life. And that's right. I don't think it would be fair on kids, adults crying in front of them. I'd hate that. What if my dad cried in front of me? I couldn't take that. Not Dad. It would mean the hurt would be too big and I couldn't get my arms round it. I'd die if he cried.

Macker's a bit different. He's still got a bit of girl in him.

All I can find is a pair of thin, white soccer shorts. I hold them up. The elastic has gone and they smell of moth and mank. I give them a good shaking. First thing tomorrow, I'll lift a pair of longs from the Discount down town.

By the time I get back, all the kids have been dismissed and there's only Macker, me and Big M left. She makes him put the shorts on. They're too big and reach down to his knees. She shakes her head in exasperation. From her pocket she gives him a safety pin, and tells him that if he can't look after himself, he'll have to be pinned up like a baby in a nappy.

It's then I notice that Macker has a fork in his hand. All this time he's had it. Must have nicked it from the cutlery tray on the table beside him. He's doubled it over and is squeezing the spring out of it.

Good on yer, pal. No blubbing left. All girl gone.
Squeeze her till she bursts.

Mac and I walk out together.

On the first, one of the snot makes some crack about
greenies, and I give him a hefty. A right cosh. It is too
much. The kid howls. I threaten to knock the blub out of
him if he goes to Mrs Dawson. We don't want another
Big Mothering.

I feel bad. I didn't mean to lather him, but I've got to
keep Macker together. Tomorrow it'll be Hodge and
Maggot and Fat Fat Jane. They'll wee themselves at him,
the pervs.

Macker is quiet. I offer him a chew, but he's not in the
mood. All he says is: 'Just wait, Jez. Just you wait. If
I don't have her.'

Sure, Mac! And if the sky fell, we'd catch a bag of
sparrows.

Then he sniffs. 'Why she do it, Jez? Why?'

He looks genuinely puzzled. Not hurt, not wimpy, but
frowning. Like she's the problem, not him.

Got it, Mac. She's the Bad Thing Big Time. But leave it
to Star.

Next morning Macker and I decide to bum off school.
But no way. She's thought of that. Hodge and Spaz are
to march MacNally and Walker to school. She's rung
Chadders. We're to meet in the entrance hall. She'll see
us off. Me as normal, Macker in his blazer and shorts,

fashion freak for the day. Macker tied and dyed, Big Time. They'll laugh at him. It'll kill him. He'll go mental!

Hodge says little on the way. He prods Macker now and again. Macker says nothing, just ambles along, but his face is hard. I can tell he's hurting, wrecked inside. He'll be bending a few forks before we finish.

Spaz is a gob-mouth, all the way down the Donkey Path. Calls him MacKnicker. MacWilly. Pees himself at that one. Tells everyone else that the girl in the shorts wets himself. Too right, Spaz, but one day you'll be planted, bottom of the canal, where wet comes in barge-loads.

We get to school and they're waiting for us. Maggot has gone ahead and spread the gob everywhere. He's got them in two lines by the gates. They're mainly school snot who are too girlie to refuse. They cheer as we walk through them. Macker looks gob-smacked. It's Hodge's big production.

We make it to the form room. Mags comes over. She's smirking. What does she know? I give her a hefty stare and she sees it's no giggle.

'Soz, Jez,' she says. 'What's up?'

I tell her. About Big Mother and Macker's knees of green. About the shorts too. She bites her lips, stop them grinning. I begin to see the funny side. The story has a percentage of giggle. Just above zero. But when I tell about how Big Mother gobbed on about cast-off kids and nappies and the rest of the mank, Mags gets dead serious. 'Woman should be locked up. She doesn't deserve to look after kids.'

'Look after?' I say. 'We don't need looking after. We need to be left alone, that's all. We're not kids any more. And we're not cast-off ones either.'

'Well, I think Macker needs looking after,' she insists.

'No, he doesn't. And anyway I'll sort him out.' I am suddenly a bit sore at Mags. She just sounds like everyone else who wants to run our lives for us. Macker is my mate, not hers.

'Well, if Fat Fat Jane tries it on, let me know. I'll cosh her one.' She gets up and wanders off.

That would be kicking jelly, Magsie baby. So you's a hard chick all of a sudden. Good on yer, Mags.

And Fat Fat did try it on. In Science. While Dimmo was dimmoing about, Fat Fat was passing around a bit of paper with some scrawl on it. Lucky, I got it before Macker. It showed a freaky-looking kid, wearing a big nappy and sucking on a bottle. There was an arrow pointing to a puddle and a pile of poo on the floor, and beside it the words, 'Macsmelly was here.'

I put it over the Bunsen and turned up the flame. Fire's best for mank. I gave her the finger. She gave me the tongue. One hot Bunsen up your lardy bum, Fat Fat, and you'd be chip dripping before you could say mushy peas and gravy.

And Chips saved the day. Miss C as always. She sent Macker to Lost Props. For a pair of half-OK longs so he could turn himself back into a grown-up. Old Mister Macker.

Or so we thought.

It was soon obvious that this was a different Macker. OK, but not OK.

I'd seen it all day, but only really noticed it, like it parachuted right into my head, down the Donkey Path on the way back.

We're halfway down, when he suddenly stops and says: 'Jez, it's going to be hard, but it's got to be done.' He's not looking at me. He's looking into the distance. Zooming the future. Searching.

What's got to be done, Macker? What this time? Blow up The House? Ram raid the Bank of England? Something simple? Easy?

'There's got to be a way,' he says, walking ahead. I can see he's talking to himself and has been ever since we left school. In fact, ever since we left The House that morning, Macker's been there, but not there. All the time he's been hurting. At times, I swear I could see it in his eyes. I've seen it before. He sort of shrinks into himself. Tries to make himself small so no one notices him. Today, now I think about it, he just went one step further. He went invisible. Went where they couldn't get him. Out of reach. Like you climb a tree, and out of harm's way, you can plan revenge or escape. From now on, I think Macker will be watching, working out his chances.

Knowing what I now know, it seems obvious that that

was the day he made up his mind to do something serious about Big Mother. He was either going to get her, or he was going to get away for good.

Later, I was talking to Star; telling him about Macker and the Big Mother Bitch that runs our place.

I ask him about girls. But he doesn't answer. Girls aren't his thing, I suppose. So, I think about Mags Wilkinson. I think she's getting bigger too. She's starting to push her blouse out. And I think her skirt is getting shorter. Or is that my imagination?

I think I can hear Star growling. Sort of friendly growling, like when you play with a dog and it talks tough. Sometimes Star rolls on his back and lets me stroke his tum. It's soft and warm.

I wonder if there are other Stars out there. Even bigger.

No way. Star's a one and only.

I wish I was like him, big as him, fast as him. Maybe I could ride him, like you see those little guys on elephants. We'd zoom through The Milky Way, and stars and comets and things would swirl past, and space winds would stream our hair backwards and we'd go so fast we couldn't breathe.

From down on earth, we'd look like a silver bullet. People would grab telescopes to have a look. Dimmo would be one of them. He'd plug his eye to the lens and stagger back, amazed. Blimey, he'd say, it's Walker, from Year 9, riding a runaway dog, an interstellar canine, traversing space at a million zings an hour. He's a wonder kid, a marvel, a miracle.

Maybe Macker could come. Star wouldn't mind. Any mate of mine is a mate of Star's. Thing is, I've not really talked to Star about Macker before. I tell him most things, but I've sort of kept Macker to myself. I know how to deal with him. I know his Ups and Downs. I think Star just wants me to carry on, sorting him out. Best way. Let the Big Dog concentrate on the Big M.

Trouble is, Mac was my twin, same monkey as me, only dafter. But now, monkey-boy's gone missing. Monkey-boy's lost. Somewhere in the deep forest, in the black jungle Monkey-Mac's vanished. If I can't find him, I can't help.

10

Bogies. Bad News

Suddenly I'm wide awake. Listening. Listening. I hear something. The door? I pull the blanket up to my chin. Hold it tight. I stare, stare into the black. No sound now. My throat begins to close. I gulp hard, swallow quietly, go dead still.

Someone's coming in! I sit up, back pressed against the headboard.

Big Mother?

'Whozzat?' I whisper.

'Sshh, Jez,' says a voice. 'It's only me, Macker.'

I reach for the lamp switch.

'Freaking hell, Mac! I nearly died there.'

'Soz, mate.'

'What's up? What's the time?'

'About one.'

'That's the middle of the night, Mac!'

He nods. 'But I need the money, Jez. I need it now.'

I frown. Macker wants money at one o'clock in the morning? Then I notice he's all dressed. Of course, he's going to Scotland. 'Doing a bunk, Mac?'

'I told you. I'm out of this place,' he says. 'I hate her. She's a bitch, Jez.'

'I know, Mac.'

So, Macker is actually going to do the bunk. He's going to borrow a quid or two, climb down the fire-escape and disappear into the Big Out There, the prat.

'And do us a favour, Jez. Destroy the Book. You got to get hold of it. Burn it or something. OK?'

OK, Mac. Me and the FBI, we'll raid Big M's secret vault, blow the safe, seize the Black Book of Bad Kids' Sins and scarper. Mission Impossible, Mac. Who do you think I am? James Bond?

I say YES because I know why he's asking. She has him down as a bed-wetter. It's in the records. As long as it's in the records they've got you. Everyone will see it. Everyone will know. Point the finger.

Well, no one's going to laugh at Mac. YES will wipe the memory. YES will clean the stain. I'll do Macker's YES for him. Somehow.

He gives me a fist.

I look at him straight. I'm tired. 'Macker, you're not serious? About doing a bunk?'

He is.

'But where'll you go? They'll only bring you back. And then you'll get the Cupboard, all weekend probably.'

'I got to get out.' His voice goes hard. 'Look, Jez, you can sit here like some dimmo rabbit if you want and let her mess you up, but I'm out. And you can stuff those mank shorts down her fat neck. I'll get a job. No worries.'

I say nothing.

119

'You think I'm stupid, like the others. But I'm not. I know something. You'll see. You're the one soft as snot. Not me. I'll surprise the soft lot of you.'

I look at him. Big talk, Mac. Slagging your mate make you feel better?

Uhhm.

Maybe he is right. Maybe I am a snot at heart. Maybe I should be more like Star – free, going my own way, sticking a finger up to Hodge and Big M, The House and all the rest of the mank in my life.

'We could ring that Childline number. The one Miss Chips gave us.'

Macker snorted. 'Load of girls! You got to do it yourself, Jez. Don't you see? They're all in it together.'

Are they?

'I've got to go,' he says, more urgent now. 'Got to go, but I need quids.'

'There's some in the end pocket of my coat,' I say.

'Right, Jez. Yer a mate. Pocket of yer coat?' He rummages around then looks up. 'I've got to do it. You don't mind, do you?'

Not-so-sure Mac's back. This is Old Macker talk. Not such a tough cookie now.

I watch him pull out a fiver.

'OK, Macker. Just go.'

'Thanks, Jez. Thanks.' He pauses. 'And another thing. I need some trainers. Mine are knackered. I'd never get to Scotland in them. Can I borrow yours for a bit?'

'Borrow, Mac? For a bit? You're going to return them? I thought you were off. Out. On the bunk. Never coming back.'

'Please, Jez. I gotta go.'

I watch him sleeve-wipe his nose. Notice his sprouty hair, his teeth all chocker, his big trembling hands. Oh, Macker m'mate, what has she done to you?

'Trainers are behind the cupboard.'

Macker looks, then turns round.

'Not there, mate.'

I frown. I get out of bed. Check. Search drawers, search the desk, try under the bed. I find a slipper and a pair of old footie boots.

But no trainers.

Freaking hell! Where are they?

'They're gone. Nicked,' I say. 'Some brickhead's had them.'

Macker looks as though he's been smacked. 'What about the footie boots?' he asks.

'Sure.'

He picks them up.

'Are you going down the fire-escape?'

Macker gives me one of his grins and shakes his head. 'I've got another way.'

'Oh yeah!'

'Yeah, but it's a secret.'

'Come on, Macker! You can tell me. We're mates, right!'

He presses his lips tight together and shakes his head. 'See ya, Jez. You won't tell, will you?' He fists my arm and tiptoes out.

OK, Mac, so what's happened? Don't trust yer old mate, Jez? I thought we shared stuff, Mac, one hundred per cent. You and me, blood brothers.

So what's up? Big Mother messed yer brains?

I think of Macker clogging his way down the fire-escape.

No, Mac, I won't tell. I won't need to tell. I'll give you twenty-four hours at the most. They'll bring you back and she'll kill you. You won't be going to school in lost prop knicks, you'll be going on crutches.

I turn the light out and look for Star. Was it Hodge nicked my trainers? Why? They were mank. From the market. He wouldn't want them. Had the police been in? Searching? Looking for evidence? Maybe they wanted to match them with footprints in the graveyard? They could analyse the soil on the soles, like they do in the *True Crime* cases that Maggot reads all the time. Then they could compare it with soil from the scene of the crime. They could get a match; and that's me down the cop shop, Dave from Social Services ear-holing me and wanting off the case, Big M spitting nails and ready to hammer me to the wall.

I stare into the darkness.

Maybe I should follow in Macker's footsteps. Take a long walk. Ring Childline. Spill the mank on Big M. I think about what Mac said. Load of girls. I've heard about kids shopping people like Big Mother. I've heard they shop SS prats all the time. Maybe. Maybe.

Then I hear Star talking. He's been listening all the time without me realizing. Thing is, he is saying, you didn't really want Macker to go, did you?

I don't say anything. I feel bad about not telling him

122

about Macker doing a bunk. About not being up front about my mate.

It's dead dark in my room, but I know Star's looking me straight in the eye.

No, I say, I didn't want Macker to go. But that's because I'll be on my own now. He was my best mate.

Star nods. Says nothing. He's letting me work it out.

I was a bit mad too, I admit. It was like *he* was just leaving *me*. He could have asked me to go with him, but he didn't. We've always done things together. It's like being dumped, I say.

Star raises his eyebrows. I think he thinks I'm being pathetic. Mags would say that. Don't be pathetic, she says. They're both right, Mags and Star. It's OK. Macker can do what he likes. Everyone's entitled to do what they want. But not if it means hurting best mates, surely. Right?

Then Star says I'm jealous. Joke. Me? Jealous of Macker? Pull my back leg. The snot might like it. Hero MacNally? Me, jealous? No way. He couldn't twock a chew in a chocolate factory.

Rabbit, rabbit, says Star.

Yes, well, maybe he will get to Scotland. And maybe he'll get caught.

Least he ain't no rabbit, says Star.

True, Star, true, I say quietly.

I pull the curtains aside. A single cloud spreads across the sky. Its edge is like the edge of a vast ice-field. Pale grey. Up there it's a Big Place. Stars light the way to infinity, says Dimmo.

123

Look after Macker, Star. He's still my friend.

Then I think of Mags. She's a friend now, I suppose. A sort of near-friend. Not really a mate. You can't have girls as mates. That wouldn't work.

Then I remember how she stood up to Hodge on the towpath, ready to clobber him. I remember how she smacked me one. I remember how she left me standing in the canal. Well, maybe Mags might make a mate after all. There are always exceptions.

Next morning, breakfast. No Macker, of course. He's on his way to tartan land. Spaz has got solitary. She must have found out about his ducking in the canal and given him the corner for it. I don't look over. He'll give me the finger if he sees me. Bad news, Jez-boy. If she keeps him back I might get to school first. School's safer than The House. More kids. More places to hide.

Stick with teachers. Disappear in the crowd. Volunteer for everything.

Hodge is head to head with Maggot and butter-slapping his toast. Maggot sees me glance over and draws his knife across his throat. Hodge is too busy chomping to notice.

One day, I'll get Maggot on his own and mix his teeth for him. Give him a dose of knuckles, as Chuffer says.

Big Mother is prowling around. There's not much talk when she's on duty.

I keep my head down and crunch on Rice Krispies. They smell faintly of wax polish. Both my hands are tinged red.

She's counting heads. Minus one.

124

'Anyone seen MacNally this morning?'

Silence.

Dozens of people must have seen him by now. A snot-nosed kid, sprouty hair, wearing footie boots and hoping to get to Scotland on a fiver won't be invisible. When the news of his escape gets out they'll set up road blocks, alert customs, close airports, seal the motorways, search train stations and derelict buildings and deserted farmhouses and marshland and moors the length of the land. The army and the police will be called out. Helicopters will survey, tracker dogs sniff sniff, security cameras scan scan. But King Macker, the boy with a thousand faces, the master of disguise, will elude them all. Go, Mac, go.

I'm in Miss Chips' lesson. Friday morning, and it's History. Macker is marked absent. Mags gives me a thumbs-up. I thumb back. We've got to write about our earliest memories. So I've got to write about The House. Why, I ask Miss Chips. She says it's history. I say I can only remember about ten years back. It's not old enough to be history. It's fresh history, says Miss Chips. She says it's my history. Everybody has a history, she says, starting from the last second, the one that's just ticked away. Last seconds? Ticks of time? They're not history. How many seconds before you get history? I dunno.

My history's boring, I say. Who wants to know? Miss Chips says she does. But she has to say that because she's a teacher. She collects history. It's her job.

I say, if we put everybody's history, all the histories, together would we get one big mega history?

She says no. If we put all the food in a supermarket

125

together would we get a super meal? No. We'd get a mess. What we need is a recipe. To make sense and not a mess, History has to have recipes. We have to know how to mix histories together so we get a good blend, the right flavour, the right taste.

She smiles.

Understand, Jez?

No way.

So I think about my history. Should I tell her all about the Bad Things? About red hands and the smell of paraffin, about wasping and ratting, and cold baths and ducking, and salt porridge and the Hand and the Cupboard and the mank of Big Mother? Should I?

Then I begin to understand what Miss Chips means about history having a recipe. The recipe for my history is called Bad Things. The only thing is, it doesn't taste good. It's like slops in your life. It stinks. Like cooked cabbage. My history is cabbage mank.

I've just started writing, when my history gets up and smacks me in the face.

First, Miss Chips suddenly wants to know why my hands look as though they've got first degree burns. I say it's polish. She wants to know, why polish. I tell her. She says it's a disgrace. It's an abuse. It's child labour.

Then some snot kid comes in the class with some manky exercise book. It turns out to be mine. Someone's found it in the kitchen skip. Miss C wants to know why it's been found covered in custard.

How do I know?

126

I do know, of course. It's from when Hodge and his lot got me in the churchyard.

Fat Fat Jane is giggling about the custard.

'OK,' says Miss C. Here she goes to her desk. 'While we're about it. These were handed in today by some honest-minded citizen.'

Miss C returns to my table, holding up a bag, one of those half see-through plastic types. Inside, there is something with black-and-white stripes on, and I know immediately they're my boots, the ones Hodge tossed up the tree, the new ones. Macker has the old ones. At this very moment he's probably practising penalties with the Celtic guys – some dream.

'Got your name here.' Miss C points inside one shoe. There it is: name and number 32. That's me, number 32. All the kids in The House have a number.

Miss Chips looks at me, frowning. 'Now, I wonder what's going on when a boy in my class leaves his property spread about the town and chucked into bins?'

Time to keep gob-tight. I just shrug.

'I see,' says Miss C. With a bent finger, she slowly draws her glasses down her nose and looks at me over the top of the frame. 'You don't know. You haven't a clue. You've never seen them before. It's nothing to do with you. It's not your fault. You've been out of the country on safari. Come on. What happened, Jez? Who did it?'

She fixes me with those smiley eyes of hers and I feel real see-through. I guess she knows it was Hodge and his gang. She wants me to say it, but that would make me a squeal, a snot. I'm not that sort of kid.

'I know it's not easy for you,' she says. 'But unless you tell me, I'll have to report the matter to Mr Chadwick. We're not having bullying in this school.' She pauses. 'Well?'

'I can look after myself,' I say. I know once I start, she'll want more. She'll get it out of me. She'll find out about the attack in the graveyard, and then she'll ask me about the fire because that's the way she works, connecting one thing with another. History is about connections – she's always saying that. But I'm not keen on Miss Chips playing connections with my life. So, I say again: 'I can sort it.'

'Can you indeed?' Miss C raises her eyebrows. 'You're not Clint Eastwood, you're a kid, Jez Walker. So stop pretending you're playing tough in some Mafia drugs bust. This is real life, and it's serious. I want to know, who did this?'

I can see she is getting annoyed because she is doing her stare and glare thing. I hate that, when the eyes pinpoint you.

'It's all right, miss. Honest. I can sort it out,' I repeat. I stretch a hand out for the plastic bag, but Miss Chips moves it out of reach.

Then Mags pipes up. Without me knowing, she's walked up to Miss C's desk.

I could have killed her.

'It's Hodge, miss,' she says, 'Jez told me. He has to live in a place called The House and it shouldn't be allowed. It's not fair. A woman called Big Mother runs it and she's a nightmare. She makes them eat salty porridge. It's not Jez's fault, miss. And he's not scared. Even though they rat his bed, he's not scared. So, if he's not scared it's OK, right?'

'No,' said Miss Chips. 'It's not right.'

'But we're going to sort it out, Miss Chips. We are. You'll see. They won't get away with it, will they, Jez?'

I just close my eyes. If Miss C talks to Hodge, he will shop me Big Time. He'll tell her I did the fire – in the churchyard. And she'll believe him because she wants to, she is that mad about the King's Oak getting burnt. And she knows I've been a torcher before. All the teachers do. It's in their records. Once you get a history like that, you've got it for life, like a birthmark. Hodge'll tell her about the twocking too, put me right in it. And all because Mags opens her big mouth.

Anyway, I start writing. I find I'm not writing about all the mank in The House, the stuff I've told Mags Wilkinson, but I'm writing about my dad and about Star, my friend. And this is crazy. Crazy for real. This isn't history. This is just the story bit. About two people who don't actually exist at all. This is not about what happens in my House life; it's about what happens in my head life.

I think about this. Head and House. I suppose if it weren't for Hodge and Big Mother then Star wouldn't have come to help me. I think he's going to do something soon. He's just waiting for the right moment.

I look out of the window. Some kids are out on the playing fields, scrapping over a ball, ignoring Sportie Higgs whistling from the touchline where he refs because he doesn't want to get his tracksuit muddied up on the manky pitch. He's a brickhead.

Then the bell goes and Mags comes over, all smiley.

'What you say all that for?'

'What?' she asks, frowning.

'You know. Squealing on me about Hodge and Big Mother and all that stuff about porridge.'

'But it's true. You told me.'

'Course it's true. But that doesn't mean you've got to go blatting about it to teachers.'

'I wasn't blatting.' She pauses. 'I don't think it's fair, that's all. I was just trying to help. I thought we were friends now.'

'I don't need any help,' I grunt. 'I'll sort Hodge out myself.'

'Yeah, with whose army?'

'I'll sort it,' I shout.

'Yeah? You some kind of hero?'

'I don't go wimping to teachers, that's what. I'm not that kind of scared.'

'You don't go because you *are* scared.'

'You're a waste of time,' I say and start to walk away.

'Are you stupid, or what! You're all the same,' she calls after me, but I keep on walking. I go to Miss C's desk, pick up the bag of boots and wander out of the room. She follows me into the corridor.

'Boys! Think you're so tough.'

I swing the bag backwards and forwards, like I couldn't care less. I'm winding her up again. I know.

130

'I'll tell Hodge you're coming after him, shall I?' she shouts.

I stop and slowly turn round. She's standing about five metres away.

'Well, shall I?'

I shrug. Tell him or not. Do I care?

'And you can have this.' She hurls a crumpled ball of paper at me. 'That's what I think of you.'

Then she storms off in the opposite direction, her satchel bouncing against her backside. The view makes me smile and I realize I'm not really mad at her. In fact, just thinking about it, I realize I shouted not because I really felt mad, but because I wanted to look mad. A girl sorting me out! Didn't look good.

I notice the scrunched paper on the floor. I pick it up. Unfold it.

It's a picture of a pop star or someone like that with a ring in his ear. I flatten the paper against the wall.

I'm gob-smacked.

It's me.

Wilko, are you crazy? What you playing at?

I look about. No one's around.

I smooth out the creases more. It's me all right. I stare at the face. It's OK, I suppose. Lips a bit big. Makes me look like Spaz, the brickbrain.

I stare down the empty corridor. In my mind's eye, I see Mags' bouncing bag disappear round the far corner.

I screw the paper into a ball, toss it in the air and give it a boot. Perfect cross. It loops up and drops behind a radiator.

*

Then I go to the bogs and have a look in a mirror. Someone comes in. I pretend to comb my hair. Yes, lips OK. Not thick. Spazzo look? No way.

I wonder about a ring. Hodge had one till Chadders made him get rid.

Then I notice a zit. Under the nose, just above the lip. A mega zit! I try squeezing. Nothing. Again. It just leaves a larger, redder patch.

Must have grown overnight, like a keggin mushroom.

It's keggin enormous!

I'm in the lower corridor and decide to go and look for Macker, and then remember Macker's Mackered off.

I'm just wondering whether to Macker off too when Miss Bonsai appears. She's half Japanese and works in the office. Her real name's Hatamuchi.

Mr Chadwick, she says, wants to see me now, immediately.

I follow. She's very small, smaller than me. Bonsai Lady.

As we hurry, she keeps looking back over her shoulder, checking to see if I'm still there.

He probably wants to see me about custard books and footie boots. Maybe it's about a new sportsbag.

As we cross the entrance hall, we pass a board of staff photographs all in lines, just head and shoulders, with Chadders at the top. He's wearing a suit and tie and looks like he's about to read the news on TV. There's a window next to the photographs and through it I can see a police car parked near the school gates. Somebody's been nicking Mr Patel's fags again.

Chadwick's office is at the end of a narrow corridor. You pass the staff toilet and the First Aid room and the copying room before you get to his door. It's always shut and you have to knock.

Lady Bonsai tap taps the door and steps back for me to enter. Almost immediately it swings open and Chadwick is standing there. He's tall and thin and frowning. No smiles. It doesn't look like a free sportsbag situation.

Then I notice the other people in the room. Definitely no freebies today, because standing behind Chadders is a policeman, and on his left is another, a woman officer. Bogies. Bad news.

11

The Cupboard

I'm told to stand in front of the desk. Chadwick calls me 'boy', and I begin to feel smaller and smaller.

I lower the plastic bag to the floor and step forward till I'm standing between the two bogies. On the desk in front of me sits a brown cardboard box. Outside, I can see kids dashing about the playground. Not a sound gets through to Chadwick's office. They seem a long, long way away.

'This is Jez Walker. From Lazarus House,' says Chadwick, giving the police a slow nod. He turns to me. 'The officers want to ask you some questions, Walker, about where you were the other night.'

One of the bogies interrupts. 'Thank you, sir.' She turns to me. 'It's Jez, isn't it?'

I nod. 'Yeah,' I say, calm as I can as if it's Macker and me gabbing in the playground. Inside my chest, I can hear the thud thud of my heart double bass Big Time. Someone's shopped me. Must have.

'Sit down, Jez.' She pulls up a chair. 'You like it at Lazarus House now?'

'No. I never liked it.'

'But you don't run away any more. So it must have got better.'

'No. I just got older.'

'You just did it for fun, didn't you? For kicks. Running away.' It was the other bogie talking now. I could hear the faint crackle of the phone on his belt.

'I was looking for my dad,' I say.

It sounded daft, me saying that in Chadders' office. Looking for a dad. I must have been a braincase then. But when you're a kid it's different. You see hundreds of mums and dads out there so you think, why can't I have one. You'd see them playing in the park, families, kicking a ball about, and you'd just feel sad and you'd want to run over, but you couldn't because you knew you were invisible. We were all Billy Nobodies in The House.

'You used to climb down the fire escape?'

'Sometimes. Sometimes, I just turned the opposite way out of school.'

I'm beginning to wonder if this is really about the hut or about Macker doing a runner. I can't work it out.

'After that, bunking off wasn't enough. You wanted more of a buzz, so you started on the cars and then the dangerous stuff – arson. You know what arson is, son?'

'Course. But I don't do that any more.'

'Arson's a serious criminal offence. That's what arson is. Ever seen anyone burnt, son?'

'Answer the officer, Walker,' said Chadders.

'Only a rabbit.'

'You know about the fire at the church on Monday night?'

'Yeah. Everyone knows.'

'Well, some kid, about your height, was seen running away from the s.o.c.' He pauses. 'You won't know what that is, son. It's . . .'

'Scene of crime,' I say quickly.

'Don't be smart with me, son.' He leans forward and I can smell the fags on his breath. 'We know you did the fire, so you might as well tell us all about it. What do you say? It'll be easier all round.'

'I don't know what you're talking about,' I say.

Then the woman starts, all friendly-like as if it's a deal – if she gives me a big smile, I give her a confession.

'It'll save a lot of time, Jez. And if you cooperate you'll get a caution and that'll be it.'

'I didn't do it 'cos I wasn't there,' I say.

'Come on, Walker,' says Chadders. 'Stop wasting the officers' time.'

'That's OK, sir. We can sort this out. Now, what we've got in this box, son, is a plaster cast of a footprint left by the culprit's trainer at the s.o.c.' Here the bogie pauses.

They are all staring at me, waiting. They want to see if I'll cry or something. No way.

'Come on, Jez,' says the woman. 'We can get this over with quickly. It's up to you. Just tell us about it. All we've got to do is search your room at the home, get your trainers and compare them with this cast.'

I say nothing. My mind's racing. Whoever nicked my trainers, it can't have been the police. They still hadn't been to my room. But someone else had. Who? Hodge probably.

Hodge! Who else?

He needed sorting out or my life wasn't going to be worth growing up for. Another job for Star.

I shrug. I'm thinking of the bogies turning up at The House. They won't find the trainers and that'll be me off the hook. But Big Mother will go mad. She'll blame me, roast me alive.

Frying pan into fire. Off the hook and under the Hand!

I say I've nothing to tell. The police leave for The House, taking the box.

Chadders gives me a lecture on telling the truth, how even kids in difficult circumstances and suffering deprivation should respect the facts. I think he means people like me and Macker. Facts are facts, facts are the truth, he says. History is facts, he says. Science is facts, he says.

Yes, I think. And The House is a fact, and Big Mother is a fact, and Hodge is a fact, and I wish they were all lies. And I wish all these freaking facts were rolled up into one big ball and blasted off the face of the earth.

And that's a fact!

At afternoon break, I bunk off. Go down the market. Pick up some fireworks. I look for the guy who does the tattoos and piercing but he's not in, so I go on to Chuffer's. He's not in either, so I hide my stuff in his cold frame behind some manky lettuces. Then I go down the canal for a think.

137

I decide it has to be Hodgy boy who's nicked the trainers. Who else? He's done my room before. He's after me. Makes sense.

I find myself wandering down the towpath towards Mags' barge. Maybe she's there.

I look through the broken window. No sign. I go to the end. The doors are still padlocked. No Mags today.

I chuck a few stones into the canal. I feel like when you miss a big match on telly. Sort of empty, hungry in the heart. You don't know where to go, what to do.

I watch the ripples in the muddy water spread out towards the far bank.

I'll have to stand in the cold or do the sorry bit again.

One way or the other, she's got me.

It's suppertime. Saus and mash. I've hardly had a mouthful when Maggot comes over to my table. 'She wants to see you,' he says. He draws his finger across his throat and winks. 'Now.'

I look around.

Hodge is staring at me. He gives me the finger. Spaz is grinning. Gobby prat. Something's up. They know.

'Now,' says Maggot, nudging me.

I shove him off and get up.

Once again, I'm standing in Big Mother's office.

She's staring at me. The pig eyes, the big white round face, the pink scalp. Then she moves from behind her desk and stands next to me.

'Despite everything I said to you yesterday,' she whispers in my ear, 'you go out and you cause more trouble. Trouble for me, for the police, for The House.' She grabs my ear. 'Are you listening, Walker?'

I try nodding, but she's pulling me up and I'm forced on to tiptoe.

'They've been here again. You think it's right for the young uns to see police crawling everywhere. Is it?'

I try to shake my head.

'No, it's not. We're a family here, not a den of criminals and perverts.'

This last word she breathes out slowly, letting it linger in the air.

She lets go my ear and moves behind me.

'This morning a member of the public rang me, disgusted. He'd seen you down the canal, leaving a barge with a girl, yesterday.'

'How did he know it was me?'

'Don't you argue with me, Walker. I rang Mr Chadwick. You were absent again this afternoon. Now I want to know what's been going on? It's some little slut from that school, isn't t?'

'Mags is my friend,' I say. 'And she's not a slut.' I blurt this out without thinking.

'So, it's Mags, is it?' Big Mother comes round to face me. 'Well, the school's going to know about this, and that lah-di-dah woman on the phone. She'll be interested in what you two have been up to, won't she, Walker, you and her Mags! Come on, you didn't go down the canal pond dipping, did you, you filthy little degenerate? What's going on? What did you get up to in there?'

She's standing right by me.

'Nothing. Nothing's going on.' My voice rises. I want to shout out a thousand nothings. I want to tell Big Mother she's a freak, a weirdo. A perv. I want to smash something, smash Big Mother. I'm not a degenerate.

'You're a liar, Walker. You're scum. You were born scum and you'll always be scum.' She has her face close to mine now. At the corners of her mouth I can see tiny crusts of powder. Her lips look skinless. I try and breathe mouth-only as the smell of earth and mould and wet leaf settles over my face. I'm trembling. I know I'm trembling, but I can't stop. My fist is clenching itself.

The huge face is right in front of mine. And her hand, two fingers outstretched. 'You were giving her this, weren't you! Right up . . .'

I never heard the rest. Didn't think, just swung. Caught the side of her head, smack! Next thing, she has me by the hair and is twisting me round. She runs me against the door and I'm held there, cheekbone hard to the wood, the warm stink of her in my nostrils and the weight of her pressing me breathless.

Then she's bashing my head on the door, and I'm grappling to stop her and I'm suddenly getting my fingers round the Hand. I can feel the hard wood and the metal bits. I'm twisting and pulling and there's a scream and a shuddering blow and I hear a bell ringing far away, fading, fading.

Next thing I know, she's just coming off the phone and I'm sitting on the floor, back to the door. I can see her legs under the desk. She is opening the Black Book. She is writing in it.

I suppose if I'd thought, if I'd not been so screaming angry at first and so fuzzy in the head afterwards, I could have had her. I should have keeled over there and then, pretending to faint. I should have groaned for a doctor. Made sure I had bruises to prove something bad had happened.

But this was another Bad Thing that was going to get away.

And now I was in the Black Book. Again!

She is reading out as she writes. 'Five thirty, 28 October. Jez Walker interviewed. Uncooperative and abusive. Aggressive attitude leads to assault of Mrs Dawson, House Mother. Appropriate restraint applied. Child uncontrollable. Further action – behaviour modification.'

Within minutes I am in the Cupboard – being modified. I am sitting, knees under chin, back against the side, in the dark. I am touching, very gently, my left cheekbone. It's sore and there's a hard lump forming. It's huge. I wonder what to tell Miss Chips this time. She'll notice. She'll ask.

Does she think I'm a degenerate?

I know it was Hodge shopped me. And now Mags is involved. Keggin hell!

Apologies Big Time.

The Cupboard smells. I take a little sniff, not wanting it up my nose, but wanting to know what it is. Whoever was here last couldn't hold it in. It's pee. Old pee. I feel sick, but it'll go away, I say to myself. Eventually smells lose interest. Ignore them and they go away. Maybe the kid was scared. Maybe she forgot him.

Some of the kids, snot probably, sneak up and bang on the side of the Cupboard. It's not funny first time. The bang has nowhere to go and it just bounces around inside and shakes you up. After that, you get used to it. Sounds get bigger in the dark. It's like you are shrinking and the world outgrows you. And in here, sounds are on their own, they stick out a mile – every little creak and sniff and giggle.

The House is a huge creature. I'm inside it. It's like those Russian dolls where you open one and inside there's another, smaller doll and another and another till you can't open any more and you're down to the tiniest, the size of a thumbnail. I'm the tiniest. I'm a tiny me inside this small skeleton which is inside this cupboard which is inside this room which is inside this floor which is inside this house which is inside this world.

Later, when I told Miss Chips about the Cupboard, I told her about the dolls, about how being in The House is like being a small nobody doll. She said we all start dead tiny, but we get bigger and bigger and eventually we eat up the world. Yes, that's what she said: 'we eat up the world'. She's well clever is Miss Chips. That's why lots of times I don't understand what she's saying. I think she was talking about growing up. She said we've got to be the big doll and we've got to hide all the others inside us. All the little bits of us, the baby versions.

It's like with Macker. I don't get what he's saying sometimes either. He talks nuts, but right in the middle of it all there's a bite of sense. And with both of them, I'm never sure exactly what I'm chewing.

It's not completely dark. I can see through the keyhole. If I hold up my hand I can see a keyhole shining on the palm.

Every so often, someone runs past and the Cupboard shakes. What happens if it overturns? What happens if there's a fire and I'm trapped inside? I imagine myself shaking the door, desperate to get out. I must, I must, I tell myself, or in the silent hunger of fire I'll be devoured.

I try and shake my head clear of the nightmare, but it won't go away. My mind has a mind of its own. It smells the burning now, hears the crackle of wood. I can see myself kicking at the doors, hammering on them. My hands are bruised, the knuckles are bleeding, shoulders sore.

Kick. Kick. Kick.

The Cupboard is really shaking now. Suddenly, the door gives. It's opening! There's a gap. It's opening up! I redouble my efforts. The Cupboard sways, the gap widens, the Cupboard begins to topple. It falls forward. I tumble with it. The door splinters inwards. Something cracks me on the head. Sparks gush into my face and flash like tracer into the vast blackness of my mind. I float noiselessly through deep space, drifting further and further from the bright earth and its burning sun.

*

I don't know whether I'm awake or asleep. It happens like that when you've been dreaming sometimes. You know you're awake, but it still seems like the dream hasn't finished. You're sort of ahead of the dream.

The House has gone silent. It has me listening. It's the sort of silence you notice. It stares at you, waiting for you to make the first move. To cough or wheeze or sniff or something. Waiting makes it worse. It's like when you know someone's somewhere in the same dark room as you and you're waiting for them to jump out and shout. You want them to jump out and shout. You know the scare's coming and you want to get it over with. Quick.

Silence is there all the time, underneath everything. It's just there, naturally, like time. We just don't hear it very often.

Silence ignores you. That's what I don't like. Big Mother's the same. She forgets you. She's forgotten me now. She's an old witch. She'll jump out at you without warning.

I start tapping the door, just gently with fingertips, just enough to hear the silence out there. Bit by bit I tap louder. Then, I turn to knuckles. I rap the wood. Harder and harder. Soon I'm punching the doors, rattling and shaking them and making a right din.

Then, suddenly, the keyhole light goes out. And it's as black as a no-star night. I stop and lean back, breathless. No one comes. She has freaking-well forgotten me.

My backside is numb, so I try kneeling. I'd stand, but there's a shelf just above me and there's not enough room to lie down. I start to imagine the walls are moving, closing in. If I let them come, they will crush me. I reach out with my hand to halt the advance. As soon as I touch wood, they stop. If I take my hand away, they will start again, inching silently inwards. I leave my hand in place. That'll stop them in their tracks. Nobody's going to squash me.

I could be lying in a coffin. In the dark, on your own, you soon start to fall apart, and your bones lie for centuries, decaying and sinking, decade by decade, into the earth.

I start thinking about Mags' house and then her mum's warm towel, and then hissing hot spits of shower water. I could smell the sea in that soap. I let the long slow shushing of waves fill the silence in my head. The dark is now a bright sky of deep creaseless blue, without a single blotch of cloud. I am running along the beach, barefoot through broad skims of water. Mags is ahead of me, skipping and twizzling and waving and doing aeroplanes.

As fast as I run, I can't catch her.

12

The Innocents

Weekend over.

After two days in The House, going back to Monday school feels like a trip out.

Police are in again. I'm back in Chadders' room.

They want to know where Macker is. Dunno, I say. They want to know where I've hidden the trainers. Chadders wants to know. So does Miss Chips.

So do I.

They've been nicked, I say. No one believes me.

In the playground, I look round for Mags. She's with some of her mates. I wander over. They turn away. 'Get stuffed, Walker,' says one of them.

'Stuff you too,' I say, frowning and not moving.

But inside I feel ... I feel ... sort of angry, but empty too. Underneath. Suddenly, I want to smash something.

I walk off. A ball rolls towards me. I watch it, time it, belt it. It sails high over the railings around the eco area and lands with a splash in the pool. Some kid, a snot probably, calls me and I chase him till he disappears in the crowd and I'm left suddenly face to face with Hodge.

He makes a grab for me, but he's too slow. I skitter and weave across the playground. He doesn't follow. 'Get you later, Walker,' I hear his voice roar through the din of kids playing.

Soon, I'm back near the girls. 'Ooh!' says one. 'Can't keep away.' It's Fat Fat Jane.

I notice Mags. She wrinkles her nose like I'm the bad smell around.

'Can't take no for an answer,' says Fat Fat.

Who'd ask Fat Fat the question in the first place? Not me. I look at her. Big mouth, big bum, big blobs.

They start chanting. Mags included.

That means she's mad, mad mad.

Fancy hanging around with Fat Fat. She really must be mad.

Before the break bell, I sneak up to second corridor and check behind the radiator. I reach down and pick out the crumpled ball of paper. I stuff it in my pocket.

Miss Chips is late to class so I sit by the window, take out my exercise book and start to write. I'm writing my history again like Miss C says. I write about the seconds, the minutes, the hours I spent in the Cupboard. It seemed like years.

By the time Miss C is back, I've written nearly two pages. She tells me to finish and sets different work for the rest. This is because she wants me to write. She says

I'm a natural. It's like Beckham's a natural. She's helping my talent 'blossom', she says.

She wants to read it.

After, she calls me up to her desk.

'Is this true?' she asks.

'Sort of,' I say.

'Sort of? Look, Jez. You've got to report this. Tell your social worker. I'll write to the woman. What's her name, Dawson? It's illegal. It's just not right.' She looks me over as if checking I'm not damaged or something. 'Have you heard of Childline?'

Yeah, yeah. Everyone's heard of Childline. Everyone's heard of the police, but it hasn't stopped kids being put in cupboards.

I don't say this. I know what Miss C is saying. They'll send somebody in if there's a complaint. Interferers. Big Mother will explode. She'll go mental. She'd kill me if she finds out.

I shake my head.

'It's wrong,' says Miss Chips. She's talking very quietly. I can hear the silence of the class, all of them listening. They know something's up.

'You know I'm going to have to report this, don't you?'

'She'll kill me, miss,' I whisper.

'No she won't. We'll have you out of there.'

'She'll still get me.'

Suddenly, Miss C puts her arm round me. Hugs me. A great whale rises up from my stomach. I'm shaking all over.

'It's OK. It's OK,' Miss Chips is saying. 'It's OK.'

'Don't tell, miss. You've got to promise. I can sort it. Honest.'

She frowns.

'And I didn't hide those trainers. Someone's nicked them. Now promise, please, miss?'

She nods and nods. 'But you've got to ring Childline. Promise.'

I shrug.

'Promise.'

I nod. Stuff Childline. This is something I want me and Star to sort out, the two of us together.

She sends me back to my table.

I'm on my own. Macker's empty seat is next to me. I wonder if he's in Scotland now. I wonder if he'll go and see Celtic.

Outside, a shaft of sun leans across the playing fields. I watch Sportie again waving at a bunch of plods playing hacker/whacker. Whack the ball, hack the other side. Sportie calls it soccer. What does he know?

Suddenly, I realize someone is sitting in Macker's place. It's Mags.

'Miss C said I've got to look after you.'

'Oh. Thinks I'm ill, does she?'

Mags ignores this. 'I know about the cupboard thing,' she says. 'She let me read your writing.'

'Well, that was supposed to be private,' I say. I am really dead annoyed, but I don't want another row with Mags so I try to sound OK about it.

'You're right,' she says, 'She's a witch. And I'm going to tell her myself.'

Hey, Mags, hold on, it's my life here. I'll make my own history.

'It won't help, Mags. Nothing will,' I say.

'Yes it will. I know it will.'

For a moment she is silent.

Then she says: 'Because there's only ten minutes left, Miss C said I could do a drawing of you. It's for Art. I've got to draw a portrait. Can I?'

'OK. And . . . er . . . soz about yesterday.'

She smiles.

'Now you've got to sit dead still.'

I hear Fat Fat Jane quietly whistling 'Here Comes the Bride'.

Mags stares at her. Suddenly she's whizzing the pencil over the pad she's holding.

I freeze.

Then she nudges me. It's not my picture. It's Fat Fat Jane with the body of a hippo sitting on a collapsing chair.

We giggle.

'Still again.'

'No big lips this time.'

Mags looks at me, eyes wide. Smiles again.

She knows.

I know.

We both know.

She wants me to meet her in the town library after school to work on the project. There's some old book her mum's found about the history of Lazarus House.

And I'm invited to tea at her place afterwards.

*

150

Tea's OK. It'll be dark by then. But the library's a prob. What if Hodge or Maggot or Fat Fat Jane see me in town with Mags Wilkinson? And then going in a library? No way.

I tell Mags I've something on after school, but I'll meet her there about 4.30.

She's OK about that. 'I've discovered something,' she says, 'about The House. It's awful.'

She won't say what it is.

Mags! Come on. Tell.

She refuses.

'Wait till this evening,' she says.

It's only afterwards I cotton on that she's making me too curious to bottle out. They really have you on, girls. Manipulate you.

Lunchtime, I'm out of the gates and down the allotment to Chuffer's. I want to get the fireworks out of the lettuces and into the hut.

I get to the allotment gate. It's tied on with string and you have to lift it, not swing it open. I pick my way along one of the paths between sprouts and cabbages and dead bean stacks.

I go up to the hut door. The padlock's off so Chuffer must be inside. I knock. Not too loud. He might be dozing. He's probably slumped in his armchair, pipe fallen on to his chest, arms tucked under his braces, nice and cosy.

I look through the window hazed with cobwebs and dust. No sign. Chair empty.

I give the door a bit of a shove. It doesn't move. I push harder and I hear the bolt rattle inside.

He must be in there. So why's the dozy git not answering? Maybe he's fallen. Had an attack.

Chuff? Chuff?

I peer through the window. Same old junk.

I run round the back. Try one of the peepholes. I'm looking into the little storeroom at the back of the hut. Nothing but a row of creosote tins and burst bags of white stuff.

No burst Chuffer.

Then I notice what looks like the edge of a mattress on the floor. Maybe he's barricaded himself in for when the eviction people come from the Council. Good for Chuff. With you, Chuff.

I try another hole. I can see through the storeroom doorway into the 'lounge', as Chuffer calls it, where he keeps the armchair and the stove and all his railway stuff. And as I'm scanning for collapsed Chuffers I see someone skip across the opening.

I freeze.

Burglar?

I back off. Creep down the side and slide behind a large mound of rubbish. It's topped with dead nettles. As I peer through them at the hut, I hear someone coming, shuffling and muttering.

It's Chuffer.

I rush out to warn him.

'You silly little sod,' he grins. 'Burglar? Who'd want to do a place like that?'

I turn round and look at the hut.

152

The door is opening. I watch as a figure steps out.
Freaking hell! It's Macker.

Over some Chuffer tea, I find out about Scotland. After he got out of The House, Macker said he hid in a park and a bus shelter. Then he tried hitching, but no one would stop. He caught a bus to the Ring Road and began walking and hitching again. No luck. By then his feet were killing. Boots were too small. So he turned back and decided to go to Chuffer's place for a few days. He said he'd never go back to The House, never again.

'Now I've got some trainers, I can be off any time. You can stay there if you like, Jez. Not me.'

'They should close places like that down,' said Chuffer. 'That woman needs shooting, a dose of knuckles. If I had me train,' said Chuff, 'I'd give you a lift. Up through Carlisle and Moffat all the way to Glasgow. Soddin motorways. When we had trains, real trains, we didn't need motorways. We didn't know how well off we were. Bloody government. You could get all the way to Glasgow for five shillin then. Now, you can't get across the road for that.'

'So you've still got my fiver, Mac?' I say.

He shakes his head. 'Bought these.' He points to his new trainers. 'Off the market.'

'For a fiver?'

'Borrowed a bit.'

Yeah, I think. 'Lifted', more like.

'Police'll have you if you get seen.'

Macker shrugs. 'I go late, when it's dark.'

He looks at me, eyes narrowing like he doesn't trust

153

me. 'You got some quids I can have? Just to get out of here.' Then he brightens. 'I'll pay you back. I will, when I get a job.'

Sure, Mac.

I remind him that the fireworks lost in the canal were part of his stash and I've nothing left over. I don't tell him about the rockets in the cold frame with the lettuce.

Well, why should I? I can play secrets too!

He volunteers to go back to the market, get some bangers, *StarBusters*, whatever.

I say no, it's too dangerous.

'One day you'll blow something up. Bloody dangerous, fireworks,' says Chuffer, lighting his pipe and coughing out smoke. 'Now, Mac, let's have another brew. Then we'll sort you out.'

We wait there till it grows dark. I tell Macker about the Cupboard and the police search. Again Chuffer says shooting and a dose of knuckles is too good for 'that woman'. Macker says he's got a better idea about how to get rid of her. He won't say what it is.

'Get out, Mac. Go to soddin Scotland,' I say. 'That's the best way to get rid of her.'

It's raining and the library lights glimmer on the wet pavement where I'm standing. 4.30. I pull up my parka hood and quickly climb the steps.

I look everywhere for Mags. Where is she?

From every table I get the old git stare. I see old git thinking too. Got his hood up – must be some kind of psycho. I push it back and start to smile instead. Old git fears confirmed. A smiling kid? Must be psycho!

I put the hood back on and try upstairs. I find her in the archive room. I look through the glass door-panel. She's wearing black cut-offs, pink top, and her hair hangs down as she leans over the book in front of her. She looks older than she does in school uniform. I wonder if I do.

I knock on the glass. She looks up and smiles.

I wait for her to come to the door. She seems taller than usual, taller than me. Bit flat too. She got heels on? I raise myself a little by standing on slight tiptoe. By the time she's the other side of the glass I'm just about her height. She opens the door.

'No need to knock,' she says. 'It's not locked.'

'It's a library, isn't it? And I always knock on closed doors.'

'Put your hood down. Take your coat off. You look psycho like that.'

Thanks, Mags.

She pulls up a chair and we sit together. No soap smell this time. But something richer, deeper like . . . like . . . I don't know what.

'Where's this stuff about The House?' I ask.

She points to this mega book. It must weigh a ton.

'It's a facsimile,' Mags says.

'Eh?'

'A copy. The original's locked up. It's called *A History of the Manor, Parish and Environs of Appleton in the County of Cheshire from Ancient to Present Times written for the Greater Glory of the Lord and for*

155

the Furtherance of Wisdom among his People by the Reverend Samuel Portrice. Good, isn't it.'

'If that's the freaking title, no wonder the book's a mile thick.'

'Right! Now see here. Page 345. Read that, Jez.'

It was a story about the plague, written nearly four hundred years ago. This was real history. In the parish of Appleton there was a Lazar House just outside the village itself. I looked at Mags. 'Lazar?'

She shrugged. 'Have to ask Miss Chips. From the rest of the story it sounds like a hospital.'

When the plague appeared in a nearby village, the people of Appleton became anxious. They heard of how plague victims swelled up with boils and buboes and then died. They saw how the sick and diseased in the Lazar House also had boils and sores. So they began to call the Lazar House a Plague House. When they heard about people nearby dying and crying out in their torment, they took counsel. It was decided by the whole village that every lazar should be confined to The House and not be let out to contaminate the air. Each one was locked up and warned: should they come out, they would be killed. The people also thought that if the plague did come, it would find such easy work among the lazars it would have no need to visit the rest of the village.

But visit it did. A baby died, pustuled and swollen.

Confinement has not worked, said the villagers. The lazars are destroying us. Only fire burneth out pestilence.

Then one night The House burnt down and all the lazars perished, sick children among their number. No one knew how this happened. The Rev. Portrice quotes an eyewitness who described how: 'the flammes were so angrie thye turned night into day. Suche was the furie of the said flammes thye flew into a corn fyeld besyde and destroied all the croppe and three goodly houses withall.'

But the villagers' crime was no protection. The plague came and destroyed them too, every one of them.

'To this day,' wrote the Rev. Sam, 'Appleton is sometimes called Black Appleton after the terrible event of that dismal night.'

'Never knew that. Black Appleton.'

'The thing is,' says Mags, 'that Lazar place was built on the spot where you live now. That's why it's called Lazarus House. See?'

I nodded slowly.

'Think of it,' she said. 'Under that House lie the ashes of the long dead. Scary, eh?'

'The long dead are probably everywhere,' I said. 'Like the old gits downstairs. It's ashes piled on ashes. You're always hearing about graves being found in farmers' fields or on building sites. Think of the millions and millions who have died down the ages since the Romans. They're all in the ground, somewhere, bits of them. I bet if you dig up any garden round here, you're probably digging up some peasant or other.'

Mags was looking at me, her nose turned up.

'Well, Rev. Portrice calls it a "a dark tragedy, A Massacre of Innocence". So you see,' she says, 'your House is built on top of a massacre. Wait till Miss Chips hears about this. It'll be great. We're going to get A-plus for the project.'

She fisted my arm, just like Macker does when we do mates.

I fisted her back, sort of easy, more a touch than a fist. It seemed right because her arm looked too thin for a real fisting. Anyway, Macker and I were used to it, she wasn't.

'What's that smell?' I said.

'It's a perfume, not a smell. It's called *L'Esprit de la Femme*. My mum says it has mystique.'

'Mystique?'

'Je ne sais quoi,' she says. 'It means mysterious, the secret ingredient.'

'In the perfume?'

'No, idiot. In women.' She stood up.

'Not girls?'

'And girls, stupid.'

'So, what is the ingredient?'

Mags shrugged. 'I dunno.' She shoved her notebook into a bag. 'Teatime,' she said and moved towards the door. 'Come on. I'm starved.'

I got up.

The bag bounced against her backside and her hair swung as she opened the door.

'Pronto, *mon ami*. This *femme* is famished.'

13

Checkmate

Later, in bed, I told Star about the meal at Mags' house. It was quiche, pronounced 'keesh'. I didn't know what was in it, apart from cheese, but it tasted good. It probably had a bit of that mystique as well.

I told Star about the Massacre, all those sick kids and the flames and the cindered bones. It happened here, I said. On this very spot. Lazarus House.

I had to put my hands over my ears in case I heard the shrieks and the growling flames. I imagined them seeping into the timber and the stone and the earth around. I know scientists find traces of distant disasters in rocks and things. Chemicals there radiate their presence for thousands of years after their passing. Could it be the same with being burnt alive? Are the bricks full of those screams? Could they ever cry out again?

My thoughts drift. I think of witches burning at the stake. Red flames blistering and shrivelling, blackening bones, bubbling blood.

I sit up, screaming.

I call Star again.

He is there. I can see him gliding over the grassy hills,

the wind combing through his coat, smoothing his fur, stroking his face to a soft sheen.

Good Star. Good Star.

I try and put my arms around him, but he's too big.

I look him straight in the eye. 'Star,' I say, 'Big Mother is after me. Hodge is after me. I'm on my own here. My friend Macker has gone. There's only this girl, Mags, left. I need help.'

I tell him about Miss Chips making me promise to shop Big M. He nods. Is he saying he knows about Miss Chips making me promise? Or is he agreeing that I should blag about Big Mother to Childline? Does he know this is going to be Big Trouble Big Time? Does he think this is a Good Thing or Bad Thing, blagging Big Mother, shopping the witch?

Then he answers. He places a big friendly, soft paw on my chest. I listen to what he has to say. I'm gob-smacked.

Listen to this.

He wants me to bunk off like Macker and torch The House.

Come on, Star! You can't be serious.

He shakes his massive head.

I'm a dumbo, a brickhead. Didn't listen carefully enough. No fire. No burning. Instead, torch The House and Big Mother in a blaze of publicity. Tell Childline, he says. Tell the police. Tell the CPA. Tell Social Services.

But she'll kill me.

Don't worry, says Star. I'm here. Forget the fallout. Remember friends. Mags will protect you.

Mags! Protection? You can't be serious, Star. She's a girl. What can she do against Big Mother?

Just see, he says. Just see.

I wonder whether to put him right about Mags.

She's this girl, Star. She's nice. Nice hair. Smells of soap and mystique. She's the one did the drawing on the wall. It's me looking crumpled. She lives alone with her mum. Dad's done a bunk. Does wicked drawings. Bit of a know-it-all. Sulks, too. Can't really help it. I think all girls sulk. It's their nature. And she tries it on. Tries to get her own way. You know, kids you along sort of, so you end up doing what you don't really want to. Got guts. Sticks up for herself. Quite tall though. Nice hair. Blonde. I prefer blondes to brunettes. Black's too dark. Blonde's good on a girl. She's OK, Mags.

At first, she was a bit pushy, got up my nose. But now, well, she's not that bad. I think it was that we just get people wrong at the beginning. Like when someone comes to the door, we don't want to open it at first, in case they turn out to be a nutcase or something.

Well, that's it. She's more a kinda friend than a mate.

She's not a Macker. He's a real mate. Not as real as we used to be. But we've still got a bond. I look after him. He looks after me, sort of.

It's not like that with this girl. I mean, would I have to look after her? It'd be odd if she looked after me. I mean, would she buy me presents and things? That would be OK, I suppose. I've never bought Macker anything. I've done him favours.

I look up. All the stars have gone, closed up. The night

161

sky is heaving with wind. Star has gone. He hasn't listened to a word.

It must be he doesn't like Mags.

I stop all of a sudden as a strange thought strikes me.

He's jealous. Star is jealous of my girl, Mags.

Then I go cold. Suppose he doesn't come back?

I search the dark sky. Nothing.

It's OK, Star. Honest! You're still the best. You're number one, Big Time. I didn't mean it. There's nothing to be jealous about. She's just a girl. It's nothing. Nothing really. Honest!

Next day, I give school and Hodge the bum. I go down the market on the firework run and make contact with Roy. I pick up a load from him for stashing at Chuffer's. I can only take a few at a time so it takes forever.

Macker disappears most of the time so he's no use to me. He's on the run, he says, and that means he's got to be careful. Got to work undercover, he says.

Undercover?

Sure, Mac. So when are you going to boot polish yer face and join the SAS? Why, a kid who wrongfoots Social Services and sleeps in allotment huts is just what they're looking for!!

Saturday's Bonfire Night and I've got a load of kids tomorrow wanting stuff. They'll pay right up front. Customer demand is high and I'll be quids in. I'll give Macker a fiver then. And maybe I'll get Mags something. I owe her anyway for hiding me on the barge. Just a thank-you sort of thing. Nothing big. Some lipstick or girl thing, I suppose. Or maybe a *StarBuster*? They're good. Lots of bright colours. Or maybe some pencils. Roy's got some good ones. Bargains.

But Star mustn't know. He'll get jealous.

Next few days I'm down Chuffer's most lunchtimes sorting out my stock of fireworks. I've too much for the trunk so I have to store the rockets under some old coal sacks that Chuffer's had since he last rode footplate full-steam all the way to Scotland last century.

I often take Fridays off and so does Hodge. He knows about me bumming Fridays and he'll be down the canal, waiting to get me. Or, now he knows about Chuffer's he'll maybe hang around the allotment.

So, that means I'm going in today.

I saw Macker briefly yesterday and warned him about Hodge. He wagged his finger. Hodge was no problem. He'd sort him out. He drew a hand across his throat. Hodge was dead meat.

Watch out, Macker. You're not James Bond all of a sudden.

And watch it, Jez, I say to myself, you're sounding like Miss Chips.

No harm in that, says Star, butting in all of a sudden.

From now on I've got to be extra careful, he says. I've got to trust Mags, whatever happens.

Course I trust her.

Something up, I ask.

But Star doesn't answer.

OK, OK. I'll trust Mags. I will. I will.

163

I pause.

You do know she's a girl, don't you, Star?

Soon as I get to class, Miss C says she wants me to go and see Chadders.

'What for?' I say.

She doesn't answer direct. 'Just go,' she says, like I've no right to ask why.

'Is it about MacNally?'

'Just go,' she insists.

What's the big secret, I wonder. As I leave the classroom, I glance over my shoulder. She's watching me.

Miss C knows something and she's not telling.

I can tell.

Chadders is waiting outside his office.

'Someone to see you, Walker,' he says, opening the door.

I step in.

Sitting behind the Chadder desk and looking a right gorm in a tie is Dave, my social worker.

He points me to a chair, then closes his eyes, claps his hands behind his head and leans back like he has a fat cigar in his face and is bossing it in some Mafia hideout.

'Well?' he says at last.

'Well what?' I say.

'I'm told you want to make a complaint.'

'Who told you that?'

'Your form teacher. True, Jez?'

'No, not really.'

164

So Miss C thinks I should shop Big M. And hitman Dave's the guy to do the judas on her.

No way.

Because I'm saying nothing, Dim Dave thinks I'm on the verge of spilling some beans about The House and stuff.

Suddenly he leans forward, panic-button eyes on me. 'Look, Jez, I know it's not easy. I don't like this any more than you do. I know on your side of the situation it gets tough at times, but you've got to understand we have our problems too, on our side.'

'But Dave,' I say, 'do we have to have sides? And if we do, aren't you supposed to be on mine?'

'Yes, yes, of course. You know I am. But we can't have people complaining all the time over nothing. It just messes everything up. Look, if you start making a fuss, then the school starts making a fuss and then the health people get involved, and before we know where we are there's a full-scale drama, press, police, the lot.'

Then he gets up and comes round the desk and sits on the edge of it, his leg dangling in front of me.

'The system's not perfect, Jez. You and I know that. We can do a bit here and a bit there but none of us can really change it.' He smiles. 'Here's what I'll do. You tell me what's on your mind and I'll speak to Mrs Dawson. OK? Keep it in the family, eh. Know what I'm saying?' He stretches. 'Just between you and me, Jez, I think she's a bit of a toughie but then you've got to have discipline. That's what it's about, discipline. One day you'll understand you can't manage a load of looselids like your lot without some blood spilling on the floor.' He ruffles my

165

hair. 'Good lad. Now exactly what's bugging you?' And he walks back to the chair behind the desk, sits down and leans forward, elbows on desktop. 'Well?' he says.

I shrug. Waste of time talking. I decide to keep my lid on. Let Star sort it all out.

Dave waits.

'Too much salt in the porridge,' I say at last.

Dave looks gobbed.

'Christ!' he says. 'Is that all? Salt? Porridge? Do I look like a food expert or what? And that's it?' He stands up. Loosens his tie. Shakes his head. 'I thought it was going to be the usual: abuse, bullying, intimidation, a bit of beating thrown in. You know, stuff you kids get from the papers so you can try it on.' He laughs, then sees I'm not wetting myself. 'Just joking, Jez. Bloody hell! Porridge! Give us a break.'

I look at Dave.

OK, Dave.

Think it's a joke. I'll give you some up-front, in-yer-face anti-kid crap.

So, despite myself and because Dave is pissing me off, I tell him about the Cupboard. Why I had to hit Big Mother, how she nearly killed me and how I was stuck in there for hours, no food, nothing.

I stop.

Dave is leaning back, eyes closed. Meditating? Sleeping? I dunno, but he says nothing for ages.

I wait.

I start to think maybe it wasn't such a good idea sounding off about Big Mother. I start remembering how Dave is always in Big Mother's office, how the two of them are probably right palsy-walsy, how he always bums a free breakfast in the kitchen, how he always talks and never listens, how he always waggles his finger in his ear, how he always carries a black case which he never opens.

Suddenly he bends forward and looks me up and down.

'You're telling me, Jez Walker, you assaulted Mrs Dawson, the matron?'

'Well, sort of,' I say, uncertain. 'But she started it.'

He shakes his head, runs his hand through his sprouty hair. 'You can't go round attacking people and hope to get away with it. It is a bloody crime, after all. If this gets out they could put you in a secure unit, bang you up with a load of psychos.' He pauses. 'And this cupboard story of yours. It's a good one but we both know it's a load of nonsense. Mrs Dawson may be a bit . . . er . . . harsh, but she's not stupid. She'd never hit a kid, I tell you. It wouldn't be worth her job to do that.'

I stare at him.

He hasn't a keggin clue. If it suited her, she'd baseball your brain, Dave. She's a psycho mega size, you prat. The whole House's psycho. It's snotful of dimmos, dropbrains, spazs, brickheads, wets, wozzecks, the lot.

Dave wags his finger. 'Take my advice. Forget this stuff about cupboards,' he says. 'No one's going to believe you anyway. They'll just think you're making it up, to get a bit of attention. Some kids do that. It happens.'

'You think I'm making it up, Dave?'

He frowns like I'm some little kid pestering for an ice-cream or something.

'I'll get the porridge sorted,' he says, getting up. 'And I don't want to hear any more nonsense about cupboards, about anything, right?'

I just stare at him.

Bastard.

He walks out without another word.

One day I'll sledge him.

Mags wants us to meet in the library later. But the manky showers are wrecked – again! So House B.O. rules, OK.

Girls don't go for B.O.

Like Dimmo says when he walks round the lab on anti-pong patrol, niffing's not for us. We should sort out our biology, he says. Deodorize. If he had his way, he'd crop-spray the lot of us.

I take lunchtime out and go back to The House.

I creep up the stairs on to the first floor. That's where the cleaners keep their stuff. I need something anti-bacterial.

I find one of their trolleys and pick up a can of air-freshener.

Then I remember Dimmo. Armpits should be anonymous, he says. So I nick some pine disinfectant instead. Squirt a splash on my hand, run it underarm. Not too much. I don't want to come up smelling new loo.

I lift a couple of Brillo pads.

As I walk through the entrance hall on the way off to school, I stop to look in the large mirror. It's on the right as you go out. In it, you can see all the way down the corridor that leads to Big Mother's office.

I check tie. Smooth hair. It still sticks up a bit at the

168

back. Shoes feel crap. I've got a Brillo under each heel. All I need is a centimetre.

I'm doing a final check when I see something moving in the mirror. It's a dark figure at the end of the corridor. It knows I'm looking. It raises a hand, the good one, and beckons to me.

Big Mother again.

She's waving a note under my nose. It's from the Attendance woman. I've missed so many days, my schoolwork is being affected. Please report to the school office, it says.

I'll be on Report.

What Big Mother says is that I'm getting to be impossible. She's losing count of how often I've come up before her. She makes it sound as though I volunteer. She makes her office sound like a visitor attraction. It's not. It's a chamber of horrors.

I am staring at the floor. Under there are the ashy bones and skulls and the undisturbed dust of the Lazarus kids. There are empty spaces in history where they should have been, like columns without their statues.

One more of these, says Big Mother, and you're out. 'I know what they say about us at that school,' she snaps. 'We breed lazy, dirty-minded urchins. No-goods. Well, not for much longer, Walker. I've had enough of you and your nasty little ways. This is the last straw. You've had too many chances. I've been over-generous with you. I've bent over backwards for you. Well, not any more. It's too late. So don't try complaining. You're out. On your way. I'm having you removed. I've only so much patience and now it's run out. You're going.'

She makes a grab at me as if she might hurl me through the window. I duck away and dash behind a chair. 'I'll call Childline,' I say. 'I'll tell them everything. I'll tell Social Services. The police. Everyone. The newspapers.'

Big Mother just stands there. Her eyes narrow. I watch the thin tip of her tongue slide between her lips. It looks bright red, almost raw.

'You're not telling anyone anything. No one believes a liar and thief.'

'I will. I will,' I shout. 'You beat me. You bruised me. You dunked me in cold water. You locked me in a cupboard.' I was breathless. I couldn't stop the words. They poured out. 'You're evil. A witch. They'll put you in prison. It's bad, what you do. We all think you're evil. One day someone will kill you. Stick a knife in you. I'm going to tell them. I am. I am.' I stand there, trembling, shocked.

She's waiting for me to cry.

Not this time, witch. This time, I'm really going to do it.

She starts to smile.

I stare at her. Suddenly I feel cold, shivery. Why's she smiling? I don't like her smiling.

She turns and goes to a cupboard at the back of the room. She opens the door and takes out a bag. A white plastic bag. She returns to the desk, up-ends the bag and out tumbles a pair of trainers.

They're mine.

'You,' I whisper. 'You nicked them.'

'Do you think the police would like these? Are you going to tell Childline about them, about how you burn things down, damage property, set fire to trees? Do you think they'll listen to a vandal, an arsonist, a liar, a thief? A degenerate? Well?'

I shake my head. I can't believe it.

'No. Nothing to say now, Walker, have you? Look, you're a child. You don't understand these things. I'm respected. I run a good house. Discipline's my watch-word. This House is a good house. This is a happy family. People appreciate that. No one's going to believe you. So, just forget all this nonsense. Right?'

She moved round the table and came towards where I was still standing behind the chair. I gripped the back tight. She had the Hand in front of her and the claw-like fingers were slowly moving in and out as she operated the slide on the wrist.

'I'm prepared,' she said, 'to overlook your appalling behaviour this once. But it's your last chance, Walker. Your last chance. Now you'd better leave for school.'

She picks up the trainers and slips them back in the bag, very slowly, first one and then the other.

'I'll keep these for the time being. Otherwise the police might find them.'

I edge towards the door. I'm looking at her. She's looking at me. I grasp the handle very carefully as if it's a hand grenade.

The silence ticks.

'And I know about the fireworks,' she says. 'Selling them without a licence is against the law. But, if you bring them to the bonfire on Saturday, we'll say no more about it.'

I pull open the door. I back out.

*

171

To avoid Hodge seeing me, I go the long way to school, down Miggers Lane, past Singh's and on to The Drive.

My mind's racing. I feel high. Just now, I could run faster than a Porsche, jump higher than Spider-Man. I couldn't give a monkey's backside whether she knows about the fireworks. I couldn't care less that Hodge has shopped me again. I punch holes in the air. I could crush a brick. I'd done it. I called her witch, to her face. I got her with the truth, right between her eyes. I told her. Now she knows.

She can't get me any more. Not ever again. All I'll have to do is pick up the phone. She knows that. I got protection. I'm safe. Witch-proof.

Witch. Witch. Witch.

I pick up a stone and flick it at a pillar-box. It hits it smack in the middle with a dull dong.

Hey, witch, I'm not dead.

Drink a cup of tea, you can't kill me.

But witches never die. Their blood is poisonous. They fang you while you sleep and paralyse you, then they suck out your insides.

I stand still. Traffic swishes past. Big Mother could eat you alive if she wanted. I imagine her mouth, rowed with shark teeth reddened with blood, opening up wider and wider, ready to devour me.

A car horn blasts me back to the pavement. I was halfway across the road. I could have been killed!

It was she who pushed me out. She who nearly had me under a car.

Never anger a witch.

*

172

Break's over.

I'm sitting at my desk. We're waiting for Miss Chips. In front of me, on the desktop, I've flattened a bit of paper. There's a message scrawled on it. 'Watch out. I'm gonna get you, Walker.' I decide to bum off for the p.m. Go to Chuffer's. Get the fireworks. Sell them off. Stuff Big Mother.

I look round to see if Mags is there. She is, scribbling away. Her hair's up. She looks different. Like a schoolkid. No mystique today, Magsie girl. I grin. Me, I just smell of mank.

I re-read the note from Hodge. I can't run away forever.

The class go hush as Miss C walks to her desk. We get in pairs for the project. Mags waves me over, but I want to stay by the window and the warm radiator. I stay put and point to Macker's seat. She shakes her head. I give the seat the thumbs-up, then pretend to warm my hands on the radiator. Best spot in the class. Sun and warmth. Costa del Sol.

Mags shakes her head again. She beckons with her finger then gives me the big-eye puppy look.

I shake my head.

She pleads, hands joined in prayer.

I reject her, palm up, like I'm stopping traffic.

Next thing I know, she's kneeling beside me, praying hands, big eyes and all.

Come on. Come on, Mags! Get up. Don't be such a wozzeck.

Then she grabs my hand and drags me to her desk.

Fat Fat Jane whistles.

I'm seething. In front of the whole class and Blob Blob.
What's she playing at?
   She says she's got something to tell me.

14

The Fight

'First,' she said, 'look at this.' She laid the paper out on her desk.

'What is it?' I said. 'A fancy door or something?'

Mags shook her head. 'I photocopied it from a book last night. One of the librarians got it for me. You know the tall one. The one I said fancied me.'

'You never told me. Must have said it to one of your mates.' I was scowling. A freaking librarian! The lech!

She nudged me. 'Don't be such a wozz. It's not as if we're . . . well . . . you know . . . more than just mates, is it? I mean,' she went on, 'it would be different if you asked me out. Or got me something, like earrings, for my birthday. That would be different. But you haven't, so that's OK, isn't it?'

I nodded. 'But we go to the library.'

She stared at me for a while, then suddenly started laughing. 'I mean out out, dumbo.'

I frowned.

'Oh, never mind, Jez. Let's sort this out.'

I stared at the print. Is this what she wanted to tell me about? Some manky old door?

'It's a fireplace,' she said, leaning forward.

Then she froze.

'What's that smell?' She sniffed. 'Pine. It's pine. Like loo cleaner.' She sniffed some more and began staring at me. 'It's you,' she said. Then her face changed from uggh to aahh. 'That's not fair, Jez. She made you clean the toilets as well?'

I nodded bleakly.

'Uggh! The witch. Have you told them on Childline yet?'

'No. Not yet.'

'You've got to, Jez. You've got to. We'll go out at lunchtime and do it.' She turned back to the print. 'This is in Lazarus House,' she said, running her finger along the mantelpiece of the drawing. She'd done her nails in pink. Go with the freaking rabbits, I thought. 'It's got a hidden stairway inside it,' continued Mags. 'That's why it's so mega. It's all in the book. You must have seen it. It's on the first floor. It was built in 1856. That's ages ago.'

'Dunno about that. There's nothing like it at The House. There's just bedrooms and the rec room on the first. There's no fireplace or anything.'

'We've got to have it in the project with a photo. Are you sure?'

'I live there, don't I!'

'OK, Jez. Only asking.'

There was a pause.

'Like my nails?' She held them up for me to admire.

'Nice.'

'They're pearlescent.'

'Oh.'

'What's up, Jez? You've got a right strop on you.'

'Soz.' I showed her Hodge's note. 'He's getting right up my nose, Mags.'

'Tell Miss Chips.'

'It's no good. He'll get me out of school. In The House. Somewhere. What am I going to do?'

'Dunno. We'll think of something.'

Good one, Mags. E-mail Superman. Get some real protection.

'By the way,' she said. 'That reminds me, there's a second thing I had to tell you. Well . . .'

'Well what?'

'You'll never guess.'

'What?'

'Hodge has asked me out.'

I stared at her, open-mouthed like a gobby fish.

'Out out?' I said.

She nodded. 'Out out.' Then she giggled. 'Might even say yes, just for a laugh.'

Bastard! Lechy saddo librarians and deadbrain Hodge. Who does she think she is? Queen of Sheba?

'You can have him,' I said.

I was choked. Freaking choked. I stood up and she tried to grab my arm. I shook it off and stalked out.

'Where do you think you're going, Jez Walker?' said Miss C.

'Jez!' It was Mags' voice.

I took no notice.

I slammed the classroom door behind me and stormed down the corridor.

177

Stuff girls!
Stuff mystique.
Stuff them all.

I scoot down the stairs and into the playground. I'm through the gates and down the Drive before I start to calm down.

OK, Hodge, I say to myself, this time we're going to sort it out for good. You and me.

I need to check on the firework stash, see Macker. I decide to take him fish and chips. He's my real mate. The only one I got now.

I remember what Star said about Mags. Trust her. Well, you were wrong on that one, Big Dog. She's one mega slag.

Then I stop. I turn cold. What if Star is having me on as well? Can I still trust my Star?

I look up and hear the wind in the trees kazooing through the dry wintry leaves. What's Star saying?

'Believe me. Believe me.'

Star, I say. How can I? She's dumped me. Dumped me for freaking Hodge. And you said she was OK. That's one big mistake.

'Believe me. Believe me,' whisper the trees.

I crash through the gate into the allotment. Hodge and Mags? What a prat I am. What a deadbrain.

In front of me on the path is an empty lager can. I tread it flat. I stamp on it. Crush it under my heel. Crush it. Then I realize I've still got the Brillos in. I rip off each shoe and chuck the pads away.

I set off down the path again towards Chuffer's patch.

If Macker's around I'll see if he wants mushy peas as well. As I approach Chuffer's place, I notice the door's slightly open.

'Macker? You there, mate?' I call.

No reply.

I push the door open.

No sign of Macker. But in one corner there's a great stash of fireworks. Prat! They need to go back in the trunk. Out of sight. He knows that, the wozzeck!

Before I can move them, something outside catches my attention. An odd noise. Not birds or traffic. Normal stuff. It's like a crack, like a twig breaking. Then I hear another.

Someone's outside.

Macker probably. I get up and look through the window. I'm just in time to see a figure dart behind a wigwam of Chuffer's French beans. I know instantly it's not Macker. Then I remember the time Chuffer sounded off about some kids from the school, three of them, snooping about the allotment: Hodge, Maggot, Spaz.

It has to be them and they've got me this time. Hodge wants me for the torching, Spaz for the dunking, Maggot 'cos he's Maggot. All of them 'cos they are freaks and wozzecks.

Next thing I know, a huge clod of turf thuds against the hut door. Another follows. Then others, rapidly, one after another. One rattles the window but doesn't break it. Chuffer won't mind. He's getting his patch weeded.

I can see they're softening me up. Artillery first, assault after. Soon, they'll start the shouting, and when they're right worked up, they'll charge.

Well, Hodgy boy. Time for a rocket surprise.

I reach down, pull back some sacking. It's *StarBuster* time, Hodgy boy. Remember the canal!

Something heavy thuds against the front wall of the shed.

I reach under the sacking where the rockets are hidden.

There's nothing there! I rip the covering away. All the *StarBusters*, every single one, have gone.

Nicked!

Hodge! The bastard.

I'm stuffed now.

A turf lump crashes through the window and spatters me with soil and glass.

I crouch down behind Chuffer's chair. It stinks of smoke and chips. I've got twenty kids coming at four and not a sparkler to share between them.

I soon forget quids as a flowerpot hurtles through the holed window and breaks in pieces against the back wall. Chuffer will go mental.

'No escape, Walker. It's you and me.' Hodge's voice rings out. 'Let's see yer. Come and say hello to your friend Macker.'

I leap up and peer through the broken window. Spaz is standing in the middle of Chuffer's patch, Macker in front of him, arm twisted up his back.

I warned you, Macker. I warned you.

'Stay where you are, Jez,' he shouts. 'They're just pillocks.'

Spaz gives him a twist and I hear Mac cry out.

'I'm coming,' I call.

I'd thought of doing a runner, like I did on the canal. But I couldn't now. Not with them having Macker. If I got away they'd kill him.

I pull the door open and step outside. Spaz has Macker round the throat now and Maggot is standing nearby holding a petrol can. It doesn't look good.

I stand still. Where the hell is Hodge?

Suddenly I hear a swishing sound and a burning, scorching pain shoots across my neck and ear. I stagger forward and half turn. This time I catch it across my hand, trying to fend it off. I stumble and fall backwards to the ground.

Hodge stands above me, a half-snarl, half-smile on his face.

In his hand he holds a whip. He flicks it again so that it cracks just above my face. I slither backwards, digging my heels in and pushing myself away from the flicker of the whip.

Next, he is dangling it above my face. I try to brush it away with my hand, try to grab it. But Hodge is too quick.

'Oh, no. Naughty, Jez. Naughty. Naughty. Time for another little lesson.'

And before I can defend myself he brings the whip

cracking down across my legs. I leap up with the pain and hop about, clawing at my trousers, trying to get at the burning beneath. It's like they've tied red-hot wires round my legs, like someone has run a saw over the skin and into the bone.

Then he catches me across the head and I fall to my knees, clasping at my hair and my ears, trying to tear away the stinging. Slowly I curl into a ball, shuddering and groaning.

I wait for the next lash, but instead Hodge calls Maggot over. 'Hey, Walker, you're just the guy for a good burn. Get it? Guy? Bonfire? Tell him, Maggot, say your poem. You like poetry don't you, Walker?'

I can hear Macker going mental, shrieking at Spaz, and I have a vague sense of them sprawled on the ground, fighting.

Maggot is leaning over me and for the first time I catch the heavy, dark tang of petrol in the air. I can just see his fat little face through my fingers. 'Bit of petrol, bit of light and it's Walker's early Bonfire Night,' he giggles.

Then I hear him unscrewing the cap.

'Hang on a minute,' says Hodge. 'Look who we have here!'

Maggot stops and looks up.

I turn to one side and peer out under the crook of my arm across the patch. Wandering over through the sprouts and manky cabbages is Mags freaking Wilkinson. She's grinning all over her face. The slag. What is she playing at?

'Hello, Hodgy,' she says, going up to him. 'Nice one.'

She puts an arm round his shoulder and he lowers his hand.

'Like a bit of whipping, girl?' he asks.

She smiles.

I just stare, all eyes and gob mouth.

What's she doing?

She leans towards him. Brings her face close to his.

She's going to kiss him.

I couldn't have been more wrong.

As Hodge pushes his lips towards Mags' face she brings her knee up right between his legs with such a hefty he is at first propelled backwards. Then he shoots forward as if shoved from behind, face screwed in agony, a slow gurgling in his throat and mouth.

I sit up, grinning and gobby at the same time.

Then I see Mags swing her arm and cosh Hodge a right cracker on the side of the head. For a moment, he staggers and then he topples to the ground, where he writhes and gargles on his own puke.

Mags helps me up. I look across the patch. Spaz has backed off. Macker is sitting in the cabbages, flexing his stiff neck.

I pick up the whip and give it a crack. Spaz turns, crashes through the beans and disappears. Ahead of him I see Maggot legging it for the gate.

'You look awful, Jez. Sorry I was a bit late.'

'Mags. Mags,' I say, chucking the whip aside and holding her face in my hands. 'You saved my life. You saved my life.'

I would have kissed her there and then, but as I lean forward the burning from the whiplash down the side of my neck is killing too much. I wince.

'You've got a wicked punch, Mags. Where did you learn that one?'

'Here.' She opens her fist. In the palm of her hand lies an oval-shaped, thick, crystal-glass perfume bottle. No need to tell me what it's called. '*L'Esprit de la Femme,*' I sigh. 'Of course. What else!'

'Couldn't find a cosh,' she jokes. 'This was the next best thing. Give him a headache he won't forget. Teach him not to mess with girls.'

Then she draws from her blazer pocket another bottle. It is plastic and full of some bright green stuff. 'Tie-and-dye,' she says, shaking it vigorously. 'Luscious Green.'

She walks over to Hodge, who by now is on his hands and knees, still coughing and dribbling blood.

Casual as you like, she undoes the bottle cap and tips the contents all over his drooped head.

He lets out a snarl, a gargle of mank and abuse, and makes a grab for Mags' leg, but she is too quick. He struggles to his feet, green fluid dripping down his face and over the shoulders of his blazer.

He begins to stagger towards us. 'I'm going to kill you for this. I'm going to kill you for this.'

Mags and I begin backing away. 'Look out, he's got the whip. Get in the hut, Mags,' I shout.

Hodge raises his arm, but a sudden wild whooping distracts him and as he turns, Macker hits him with a shoulder charge that sends him crashing to the ground. Instantly he is on Hodge's back, tearing the whip away and pushing his face down into the dirt and holding it there till he starts writhing for air.

'OK. OK, Macker,' I shout, grabbing his arms and trying to pull him off. But no way. He is going mental. 'You'll kill him,' I shout. I am astonished at how strong Macker is. 'Stop. Stop. Help us, Mags,' I call.

It takes the two of us to drag Macker off. We are all exhausted, and sit, the three of us, gazing at the slumped form of Hodge, now on his back, breathing hoarsely, his green fingers slowly curling and uncurling in the grass.

'Should have let me, Jez. Should have. I wanted to kill him. Whipping people like that. It's what he deserves. They all deserve it. Him and Big Mother and that slob, Spaz. And The House. That one too. We should kill The House. All of it.'

I stare at Macker. He sounds wild, but he doesn't look it. His eyes are calm, still, his expression flat.

I hadn't realized how strong he is. But looking at him now, I can see he's as big as Hodge. I'd never noticed before. He was always a bit of a slouch, dragging his feet, bumping into things. Somehow, in the last few days, he seems to have grown. I realize it now. He's got himself together. Changed inside.

I stare at him.

This isn't our off-the-wall Macker, scared Macker, somewhere-else Macker. This is someone burning inside, with anger, a killer-fire Hodge has managed to light.

*

In the end, Macker dragged Hodge to his feet, pushed him towards the water-butt, dunked him and sent him, spluttering and swaying, back through the cabbages.

Mags wanted him to come and stay at her place. She said they could sort something out with the authorities. But Macker would have none of it. He was going to squat either with Chuffer at his house or in the hut till Bonfire Night, and after it was over he was off to Scotland. Start a new life.

'Why don't you go now, Mac,' I say, 'before they find you?'

He shakes his head. 'No, I'll wait for the Big Fire. Then.' He points across the allotment, in the direction of the town, the motorway and the North.

Then I remember the missing fireworks.

15

Big Mother Coshed

I tell Mags about the *StarBusters*. 'Fifty quid's worth.'

'Fireworks?' says Mags. 'You've got fireworks here?'

But I'm not answering. I'm rushing into Chuffer's hut to check the trunk.

I pull back the lid.

'Fifty quid's worth?' says Mags, stepping in and standing next to me. She looks down at the trunk. 'Are these yours?'

I nod.

'Where do you get the money for all that?' She stops and looks hard at me. 'Is this OK stuff?'

I say nothing.

'Stolen?'

I shake my head.

'Is it safe in here? Don't you need a licence or something?'

Mags, just now I need a miracle! And someone to strike Hodge dead.

Then I explain. About Ron on the market, about stashing it at Chuffer's, about flogging it to kids and snot. 'And that freak Hodge has nicked all the rockets. Sold them by now, the bastard.'

I give the shed wall a right kicking.

'Still,' I say after a bit, 'I've got that lot left. It's something, I suppose.'

Mags, who's been kneeling and checking through the trunk, looks up.

She shakes her head. 'No you haven't. These are useless. Look what someone's done.' She hands me a large cone, a *Silver Fountain*. 'Shake it,' she says.

It's light as a feather. I untwist the blue touch-paper, turn it upside down and shake it like a salt-cellar. Nothing falls out. The powder's been emptied.

All the others, *Roman Candles* and *Fire Showers*, the lot, are empty. We check every one, including the stash in the corner. They're all useless, worthless.

Then I remember the ones in the cold frame. I rush out. Sod it. Rain's got in. They're mank.

All this time Macker has been standing in the doorway.

That's it, Mac matey. I'm up to it in mank now. I owe Ron. I owe a dozen schoolkids. I owe most of The House snot.

Mags says nothing. I know what she's thinking. I can tell by the look on her face. She's thinking I'm a right prat, trying a scam like this.

'Why would Hodge empty fireworks?' she says at last.

I shrug. 'Dunno. Make it look like I was selling kids duff stuff, put me in the mank when they snotted to the police or Chadders or Big Mother or the SS. I could get a right kicking from just about everyone.'

I guess Hodge, Spaz and Maggot had got into

188

Chuffer's hut because Macker had forgotten to lock it up. They probably had the place staked out for ages. I don't like to say all this 'cos, well, my mate has just saved me from a real work-over and given Hodge, The House psycho, the lathering of a lifetime.

'Don't worry,' says Macker suddenly. 'Whatever happens, I'm going to sort it out. Trust me.' Then he gives me the strangest look, like he is searching right into me. Like he is asking for something.

'Remember, whatever happens, we're mates. Right?' he says.

I nod. 'Of course, Mac. Always.'

Mags is frowning. Probably wondering, like me, what Macker is on about.

Suddenly she turns to him. 'You better go,' she says. 'Because the first thing Hodge'll do now is tell Big Mother you're here.'

He shakes his head. 'Got another hideaway,' he says. 'No one will catch me.' He turns. 'You going to be OK, Jez?'

I nod slowly. My scalp suddenly feels tight and tingly.

'Sure you are?'

Sure I'm sure, Mac. This is my one-time dippy, loopy mate. First, he's laying hefties on mega tough kids, then he's giving some serious people the two-finger run-around. Now, he's big brothering me all of a sudden. Strange.

'I'll sort him,' said Mags.

We arrange for all three of us to meet on Sunday morning after Saturday's bonfire and get Chuffer to do us an egg and bacon breakfast before Big Mac takes off for Scotland.

As he leaves, Macker turns in the doorway. 'Sometimes,' he says, 'you have to do Bad Things for the sake of one Good Thing.'

Mags and I leave the allotment by the back way, both of us wondering what Bad Things Macker's on about.

'What'll happen if you don't pay this Ron guy off the market?'

'He'll snot me to Big Mother. Or . . . I dunno.' I didn't like to think. Ron was OK but he was a big guy and he could easily dip me in the canal like a tea bag one minute and squeeze me dry the next.

'Leave it to me,' said Mags.

I smiled. Sit back Jez, M and M are going to sort your life out. And good luck to them, I say.

'Look, Mags,' I say, stopping for a moment. 'You were ace back there. And thanks.'

She smiles. 'Huh! That's girls for you.'

When she saw my head, her mum wanted to take me to the hospital.

I said no way. If Big Mother found out, it was public execution no reprieve.

So she gave me some emergency treatment, massaging some herbal doo-dah into the red scorch marks crisscrossing my neck and scalp.

I told her about Mags and how she'd bricked this big bully kid called Hodge.

'Mags did that?' she said, all her face frowning at once.

'Yeah. Gave him a right coshing.'

'Coshing? Coshing? Is this how you carry on in that House place? She used to keep hamsters and she loved little kittens. Any animal.' She stopped rubbing and looked hard at me. 'Coshed? Mags? Next thing I know, she'll be throwing eggs at policemen and chaining herself to trees.'

'No. No, Mrs Wilkinson. No way. Honest. She's dead nice. She never gets into trouble. If it wasn't for Mags, I'd be streaky bacon all over. When she just turned up and slammed Hodge you could have flattened me with a feather. Really. It was a right hefty.'

'Hefty? Well, I don't know where she gets it from. Her dad never had it in him.'

After supper I went straight to bed. There was no sign of Hodge in the dining room, but I did see a sick tray going up to top floor where his room was.

The police were at supper, asking again had anyone seen Macker. Head-shakes all round. Me? Seen Mr MacNally? No way.

Later that night, I lay gazing at the starry night. I could feel Star very near. His breathing was ruffling the ivy outside. All I had to do was reach out of the bed and I could have stroked his head. But I didn't. If I touch Star I'd be scared he might not like it and go away. Not everyone wants to be touched.

I told him he was right about Mags Wilkinson and that I was wrong. I was surprised she had the strength to wop Hodge one, because her arms are quite thin at the top.

Star said nothing.

I wanted to know how we were going to sort out Big Mother. Star wouldn't say, but it can't be long now.

For ages I stare at the speckles of distant light. I begin to feel uneasy. I don't think Star will stay around much longer. I can't hear him any more. I don't know why, but I have this odd feeling he's going do a runner. Bum off soon to another planet or something. Recently he's been very quiet. He goes off for long periods on his own. I wonder if this is his way of warning me, preparing me for the day he leaves.

My legs are throbbing and my scalp is tingling. The herbal doo-dah makes me smell of the goo they put in the lavs.

I can't imagine him not being around any more.

Suddenly I'm sobbing and sobbing. Don't go, Star. Please. Don't go, Star. I don't want to be on my own. Stay with me, Star. Stay with me.

Out there, in the soundless darkness, my words find no echo.

Breakfast, Saturday. November 5. Bonfire Night.

No one is speaking. No one is moving. Every one of us has eyes on Big Mother. Big Mother has eyes on all of us. She's reaching into us, feeling for our feelings, stripping us of thought.

She is speaking very slowly, like she is injecting the words deep into our veins, into blood itself.

'Someone has betrayed us,' she says. 'Someone has gone behind our backs and betrayed us all.' She starts to walk, very slowly, between the top two tables. 'Someone here is a Judas. We have a Judas in our midst.' She stops and searches round the room.

It is soundless, motionless.

A Judas?

'We are going to be inspected.' Big Mother says the word 'inspected' like it tastes of puke. 'Inspectors,' she says, 'are coming. Interferers. Poking their noses where they're not wanted. All because of some person, some cowardly snitch.'

Then Big Mother's voice begins to tremble. 'That person has reported me. Me!' She stretches the 'me' out, like she's doing doh, ray, me in music.

She pauses. 'To the authorities. Someone has told them this is not a happy House. They are lying. This is a happy House, isn't it?'

No one moves.

'Isn't it?' she shouts, slamming the Hand down on a tabletop, rattling cups and cutlery and every little snot sitting there. 'Isn't it?'

Everybody nod and nods.

'Say yes,' bawls Big Mother.

'Yes,' we all yap.

'This is the best House you'll ever have. I want you to know that. Happy is this House. God blesses this House. Every day. Now,' she pauses, 'now someone, someone in this room, sitting at our table, enjoying God's provided has cast all this aside. Who is it flying in the face of God? Who is it so treacherous that he would sell us out and destroy everything good, everything we have built together in this blessed House?'

She's mad. Big Mother has finally flipped. I watch the other kids. Most of the snot are stunned and look as though they've been hefted with a mallet each one. Spaz is frowning. Maggot's slumped in his seat, yawning. If Big Mother sees that, Maggot, she'll swallow you whole.

I am staring at my plate and the toast lying there heavy with jam and missing one neat bite. Something warns me to watch out. I look out of the side of my eye. She is slowly drawing nearer to my table. She is growing bigger and bigger. Now she is standing behind me, massive, silent like a giant statue.

'Stand up, Walker.'

I push my chair back. As I start to rise, the Hand grabs me by the shoulder and swings me round.

'Aarrgghh!'

The fingers claw me, and down my neck the whip marks burn.

Her face is close to mine. Her breath smells like gas. 'It was you, wasn't it?' There's a poisonous hiss in her voice. 'Admit it. Tell the truth, Judas boy.'

She starts to shake me.

'No. No. No.' I grope around the table behind me with my left hand. My fingers wrap round my mug.

Someone is shouting. 'It was him, miss. It was. Him and MacNally.'

Big Mother stops the shaking. Looks to the back of

the room. Everyone is doing the same. I twist round to see who it is.

Maggot. The runt.

He's jabbing a finger at me. 'Judas,' he mouths. Then he sits down.

Bastard Big Time.

Big Mother turns back to me. Her face is close to mine, and above her top lip I can see a line of black hairs. For a second or two nothing happens. There's not a sound, not a movement in the room. Then, she starts. Shaking me again. One, two, three, like she's trying to empty the bones out of me.

My fingers wrap round the mug, and in a slow arc I bring my arm round and smash it against the side of her head. I feel the mug crack in my hand.

She grunts, lets go of me, steps back a little, swaying gently, the good hand pressed to the side of her head. Her eyes are shock-open. I hold my breath. Maybe I've killed her. My heart is pounding. I think she's going to fall, but she doesn't. No. She shakes her head, stops and then, her face twisting in anger, she flies at me again.

I'm ready this time. I dash to the right, knocking chairs to one side, and rush towards the kitchen. Kids duck out of the way, and I reach the serving hatch. I leap on to the ledge, slide through, feet first, and land with a thud on the tiled floor.

One of the cooks shouts at me, and I dash round a row of ovens, through a door and into a freezer room. In the wall facing me is a wooden door. I grab the handle and yank it open.

I'm in a kind of storeroom. From a corner, where

there's a stash of them, I grab a broom and use the handle to jam the door shut.

I lean against the far wall to catch my breath, and look around. Above me there's a row of narrow ceiling-high windows. Pale sunlight is shining through and glinting on rows of large tins, stacked on shelves either side of the door opposite me.

To my left, there's a deep recess, and I peer through its arched opening into an area about the size of a small bedroom. It has a tiled floor sloping steeply towards the back and no visible ceiling, just badger-hole blackness.

I can, however, feel a chill of air, blowing gently over my face, as if it is being sucked up into the darkness to escape through some opening or other. No exit for me though.

Suddenly the door starts banging.

'Come on. Open up. Open up.'

I don't answer.

'We know you're in there. Now open this door.' It sounds like one of the cooks.

It has to be the windows.

They're about three metres up and well out of my reach. Above them is the heavy-beamed wooden ceiling, flaking white paint and hung with the dusty, broken netting of a thousand spiderwebs.

The central window is the largest and seems to be hinged at the top and it looks as if it will open outwards. Through the dirty glass I can see bits of foliage. It's my only chance.

From the nearest shelf I lift one of the big drums. It smells like floor polish and is probably that red wax stuff, The House B.O. I place it on the stone floor below the window. As I lift the second drum, I accidentally knock over a red plastic container, one of a number in different sizes hidden at the back of the shelf. I quickly put it upright because it's spilling out fluid. At first I think the smell is the wax, but I suddenly realize that what I've spilt is petrol.

'Come on, Walker. Open up. Nothing's going to happen to you. Promise.'

I need to get out quick, but be careful with it. One spark from dragging the heavy drums over the stone floor and I go up in an early bonfire.

Gently I lift the second drum and roll it slowly across the floor. I place it gently on top of the first. I need another two to get me within working distance of the window and two more after that to give me a step to climb on to the top drum.

I go back for the last one, and as I drag it from the back of the shelf I notice a large round tin shoved right in a rear corner, a tatty jacket and a bundle of what looks like old clothes.

I place the drum into position and go back. The clothes look like they've come from the Tide-over cupboard. But what I'm really interested in is the tin because it's a good size for a first step. It turns out to be one of those deep biscuit tins, and I start to open it, hoping it's full of chocolate digestives and not those manky round pimply ones you get at Patel's.

I take off the lid and stare at the contents.

It's not full of either.

It's not even full of biscuits. No, inside it's packed

with this grainy stuff that looks like ground pepper, but doesn't smell like it.

Then it hits me. I remember where I'd seen the red petrol can. It's the one Maggot was carrying at Chuffer's patch when Hodge threatened to torch me.

Then I realize where the grainy stuff has come from. It's the missing powder he's emptied out of my fire-works.

I've found Hodge's stash hole. After I'd burnt his hut down he must have looked around for somewhere else and found this place, right under Big Mother's nose. He either sneaked it through the kitchen at night or got in through the window.

I look up at the wall just above my pile of drums. There are scuff marks there all right. You can see them clearly, once you look, places where the old whitewash has been rubbed off.

'Jez, this is Dave. Do you hear me? You can't stay in there all day, you know. You might as well come out now. It's OK. Nothing's going to happen to you. It's perfectly safe. Trust me.'

No way, Dim Dave. You're a Social Worker. You're on the other side. You're Big Mother's boy. She's prob-ably standing next to you right now, claws flicking in and out.

It wasn't that hard. The window opened outwards, and I soon scrambled through and found myself crouching behind a huge holly bush. Tied round its trunk, just above the ground, was a rope. It lay in a coil beside the window. Obviously that's how Hodge and Maggot get into the storeroom below. The opening's far too narrow for Spaz. He probably keeps nix, the wozzeck.

I'm at the back of The House and decide to edge along the wall to the end. Once I get there, I stop and listen. Nothing much. I poke my head round the corner. The fire-escape looms above, and I notice the ladder is down. Beyond, I can see the edge of the bonfire where a workman – someone from the Council, because he's wearing their green jacket and trousers – is stacking wooden pallets against the base.

No one else is around, so I make a dash across the lawn, under the big trees and on to the Donkey Path.

Then I run. I don't stop till I get halfway up The Drive.

And there I stop, in a freeze-frame moment, because it suddenly hits me. What I've done. I've coshed her.

Coshed Big Mother.

Me, Jez Walker. I could have killed her.

I start to shake. I feel a tad faint. My heart's a fist banging to get out.

I'm next to a park so I decide to find a bench and flop for a bit.

I think of the hefty I gave her and the crackle of the mug in my fingers. She didn't fall. Didn't seem to feel it. Tough as Tyson, Big Mother. Sledge her and she doesn't even wobble.

Suddenly, a police siren, car attached, screams up The Drive. I shrink into the bench. Merge with the scenery, said Chuffer. Go invisible. I look around. Bushes and trees and shrubbery and one small pond. Perfect for ducks. Bad for kids on the run.

I listen to the siren's distant whine. It's dying away, vanishing into the undergrowth of Appleton. Into tunnels, underpasses, traffic lights, cranes, multi-storeys, allotments, poles, cones, bins, mank.

I'm still blowing hard, sicking up the fear and the trembling in deep breaths.

She'll be mental. She'll be banging the table, frothing and freaking out the snot. She'd have them all in The Cupboard if she could – a stash of kids: the no-hopers, hand-me-downers, raff, cast-offs, dimmos, second-handers, goms, scrag-ends, and all the bum-mank of the world, the bin-slop, the barrel-filth.

Well, not me, mate. I'm out of it. I'm flying. I'm over the horizon. No perspective, me. I'm going to hit vanishing point.

Then, I think of the bonfire. It's going to be a real cracker, a monster.

I can see the flames jumping up and grasping for air, crackling and spitting and snarling and ripping the night red. I can feel the scorch on my face, smell the smoke-breath, hear the rockets roaring to the stars.

I've got to move. It's going to be the biggest. I've got time. I'll sneak in, watch from under the trees. No one will see me.

Then I'll hit the horizon with Macker and Star.

I hear a car tyre squeal and I turn quickly. Through the undergrowth and the railings I see the hot red brake-lights.

Star eyes. He's prowling. He's looking after me. His eyes burn, burn.

16

History's a Mess

I'm walking down near the park pool, thinking hard. Who, for instance, shopped Big Mother? Macker? Could be. That's why he's still hanging around; wants to see some blood.

More likely mine'll be on the carpet. Twenty cooks and kids, big uns and snots, witnessed me cosh Big Mother Mags style. When they catch me I'm in for it Big Time, whatever dizzy Dave says.

Need to lie low for a bit and do some more thinking and get warm. I've no coat on, and a kid in a summer-white T-shirt in November isn't nab-proof. Chuffer would go mental, choke on his best baccy. I decide to go to his hut and see if Macker's the one dropped the gob on Big M.

No one there. Door locked. Chuffer has tacked a patch of plastic bagging over the smashed window.

I watch a squad of pigeons practise fly-past over the allotment and do one or two tumblers for fun. I am just about to go down the canal when Chuffer puts in an appearance, shuffling like a big ape down the path between the French beans.

'Heard about that hooligan giving you a proper belting,' he says as he approaches. 'He needs a dose of knuckles, that one. Ought to have his backside taken off. I know what I'd do to him. In my day, Jed, we had the army. Bit of discipline. Kicked you into shape, it did. They were right brutes, some of them sergeants. Brutes. See that,' he says suddenly, shoving his fist up to my face. 'The knuckles. What do think of that?'

I shrug. They look lumpy, and one is missing.

'Big buck sergeant did that. Got me with his swagger stick. Smashed the hand, just 'cos I'd nicked a packet of smokes illegal like. It stopped me puffing fags, Jed boy.' We were both standing outside his shed. He raised his hand and gently thumbed aside part of my hair. 'Ought to have his fingers broken for this. Does it hurt?'

I nodded.

'Heard a girl sorted him out in the end.' Chuffer shook his head. 'I dunno what they make lasses out of these days. It must be all them additives. In food. Makes them more like boys. You know what I mean? Wasn't like that in my day. Kept us apart, they did. Boys one door, girls the other. I was eighteen before I went walking out. Mind, there were some forward ones even then.'

He started fumbling with the padlock.

'Better come inside and get that stove going. Where's yer coat? Some thieving hooligan's had mine. Can't find it anywhere. You seen it, Jed?'

He shuffled into the hut, not waiting for an answer.

'I remember one fast miss. Jessie was her name. Little tart. Come in. Come in.' He wandered round the hut, moving this, checking that and all the time mumbling

202

away. 'Never give in to a woman. No. All they want to do is control you. Your life won't be your own. Nag yer from pillar to post.' He stopped in front of me and waved his empty pipe in my face. 'Why do yer think I come down here? Only place I can call my own. A man's got to have a bit of freedom. Can't spend all his life washing up.' He stared at me suddenly, as if surprised I was still there. 'What do you want, lad? You don't normally come this early.'

I told him about the fight with Big Mother at breakfast, back at The House, and about how I'd escaped.

'Bleedin' hell, Jed! Is there nobody you don't scrap with?'

'Macker and I never scrap,' I said.

'Hey, now where is that lad? Not seen him for a bit.' Chuffer shook his head. 'Kids! What they get up to these days.'

He lit his pipe, puffing and blowing and creating such a fug I had to go and stand by the door for air.

Macker? I wondered if I'd ever see him again. All I had now was Mags Wilkinson, and she was a girl.

'This lass, your girlfriend is she?' Chuffer was saying.

'Dunno really.'

'Dunno! You'd better get it sorted, lad. Or she'll have you running round her little finger before you can say knife. Is she . . . er . . . a bit fast?'

'Fast?'

'You know. Frisky. Forward-like.'

'No. Mags is just a girl.'

'Then watch out, Jed. They're the worst. All innocence. Don't say I didn't warn you.'

Chuffer was like that. Always warning and whining about this and that.

I watched him rummage around, grunting old git talk. Eventually he went round into the store at the back. 'Funny,' I heard him say. 'You seen my can of pink, Jed?' he called.

'Pink?'

'For lighting the stove.'

'No.'

Chuffer reappeared. 'I bet it's that whip boy lifted it. I'll give him some whipping, I will.'

If I'd told him I'd found his can in Hodge's little hideaway at The House, he'd have been up there, wanting his bleedin' property back or else. I was in enough mank without having Chuffer stirring it further. So I said nothing.

I looked up.

He'd stopped and was staring at the wall behind the stove. 'Had me soddin coat as well,' he growled, jabbing with his finger at the empty hook like it was to blame. 'Bleedin yobs.'

Yer right, Chuff, right yobs.

In the end, because the Gaz was on the blink we had to make do with the wood and coke on the boiler for the cuppa, and it took over an hour before we could get enough heat to boil up Chuffer's old black kettle. 'On the fire-plate, used to take five bleedin' minutes to get a brew,' he said.

He was sitting in his armchair, mug of tea in one hand, cold sausage sandwich in the other. 'Well, Jed, what you going to do now you're a runaway too? They'll be out looking for you.'

'I'll just sit it out for a bit.'

'So will they. They know it's hunger drives you in. Here, have a bite.'

Time dragged. Chuffer pottered about on his patch all morning. I read some old newspapers, listened to the radio and kept out of sight. I was hoping against hope Macker might turn up. I couldn't really imagine him gone for good. But no sign of him by lunch, so I decided to try Mags' place.

'Keep out of view,' said Chuffer. 'Use camouflage. Remember, you can hide in a crowd. If they come asking, I'll send them into town. Good luck.'

I grinned inside. Good old Chuffer. Where did he think I was going – behind enemy lines?

Camouflage? Catch up, Chuff.

It was late afternoon when I got to Mags' house. She wasn't exactly knocked out to see me. She wanted to go down the library and do some more research on Lazarus House.

'So how can I, with you on the run?'

'I'm not on the run. Saturday's a free day. We can go where we like.'

Mags shook her head. 'You've just told me you coshed that Big Mother woman. How do you know you didn't injure her?'

'Come on, Mags, I stunned her, that's all. She's tough

as bricks. Anyway, she's clobbered me enough. Time she got some of her own back.'

'Sure,' said Mags. 'But they could still try and get you for assault or something.'

'Listen who's talking,' I said. 'You're the one who's just crotched a kid and bricked him.'

Mags grimaced and bit her lip. 'I know. I know. Do you think he'll be all right? Nothing'll happen, will it? I didn't mean to injure him, just stop him hitting you.' She reached out towards my head but flinched from touching me, as if she thought I was badly wounded. 'Does it still hurt?' she asked.

'Stings a bit. That's all.'

'Well, I think he deserved the damage. In fact, I wish I'd given him another.'

'Thanks, Mags. I think you did a good enough job as it was. You've bodged Hodge.'

She laughed.

Nice laugh, Mags.

I laughed too. It was catching.

'Hodge bodged,' she giggled.

Soon we were both away, sliding down the wall and unstoppable. Eventually my ribs ached too much and my scalp began to sting.

'Let's have a Coke,' said Mags.

I thought only Macker and I laughed like that. I remembered the last time, when he found the rat sock.

I told Mags about it, but she didn't really get it. 'That's disgusting,' she said. 'An old sock! What's so funny about that?'

Dunno, I thought. Maybe she's right. It doesn't

sound that funny now, but it was at the time.

'So how did you get out without being caught?' she said in between sips of Coke.

I explained how I had run through the kitchen and bolted myself inside a storeroom. I told her about the powder tin and about Maggot's petrol cans.

'What would Hodge want with a tin of firework powder?'

'Wanted to make his own and flog them to snot for a mint,' I said. 'But now some girl's crocked him up and he can't manage it,' I grinned.

'Dangerous, playing with fireworks,' she said.

'Dangerous, playing with girls.' I winked.

'Hum,' said Mags. 'Not like fireworks.'

'Oh, I don't know,' I said. 'They both explode.'

'Ha, Ha. Jez Walker.'

I grin. 'Fireworks are OK if you're careful.'

'Well,' said Mags. 'I'm going to the bonfire. You can come with me. It looks like you're going to need some protection.'

Protection! Nice one, Mags. You may be cosh queen, but let's be serious here. Have you seen Big M in mental mode? You can have a gobful of mystique, you can be up to your eyes in mystique. It won't stop Big M. No way.

'We'll have to be careful. If Big Mother . . .'

Mags interrupted. 'Don't worry. She can't do anything, not if inspectors are coming in.'

I stared at her.

'Mags,' I said slowly. 'How do you know about the inspection?'

She shrugged. 'I think I heard my mum say something about an investigation or something.'

'Come on. How would your mum know about such a thing?'

Mags put her glass down. 'Well, we had to tell Social Services after the Cupboard thing. We couldn't let them get away with it. That was the last straw.'

I stood up. 'Hey, Mags! I've just become runaway boy Big Time 'cos of you. She blames me. Thinks I shopped her. That's why she tried to shake my teeth loose at breakfast. That's why I had to leg it.'

'Oh, Jez, I'm sorry. Honest, I never meant . . . I mean . . . I never thought she'd blame you or any kid there.' She bit her lip.

'Now I've nowhere to go,' I said, rubbing it in a bit.

'You can stay here. I'll ask my mum. She won't mind. She thinks Lazarus House is the pits and ought to be pulled down.'

'Thanks.' This time I meant it. I was thinking of soft towels and hot showers and L'Esprit de la Femme. It sounded good to me. 'You'll have to talk to Dim Dave. He's my prat social worker. But he won't want to do me any favours.'

'Mum'll sort him out. Once she puts her mind to it, nothing stops her.'

Now I knew where Mags got it from.

'Oh, by the way,' I said. 'While I was escaping from the witch's house I discovered a secret passage. It's like a chimney shaft and starts from the kitchen storeroom and goes up, I don't know how far. And the floor slopes up into a dark space.'

208

'It's all part of the old heating system,' said Mags. 'The dark bit is the bottom of the ash chute. In the old days they just shovelled the cinders and stuff from the dead fires down the chute into the ash pit.'

'How do you know all this?'

She ignored me. 'And could you feel a draught going up this secret passage?'

'Sort of.'

'Thought so,' she said. 'Secret solved. It's not a chimney. It's just a way to draw air up into the fires above and get the flames really going. It probably connects to that fireplace I told you about. I got all that from the library. That's history. Now I'm going to get ready. I'll be back in a min.'

I don't know why, but all that Mags is telling me sticks in my mind, like something sticks in your throat. You try and get rid of it, but it won't go away. 'There's something not quite right here,' I keep telling myself.

Then I remember what Miss Chips said once, about mess and recipes and history. 'History's a mess,' she used to say. 'A million facts all mixed up. All those people arguing and building and destroying and wandering and inventing and digging and making and doing and dying. All those lives criss-crossing and bumping into each other. It's all too much. What we need is a recipe. To make sense of the mess, History has to have recipes. We have to know how to mix histories together, so we get a good blend, the right flavour, the right taste.'

I remember thinking hard about this.

Now I'm thinking about it again. How my life now is

in a mega mess. The Hodge mess, The House mess, the Big Mother mess, the firework mess, the Chadders mess, the police mess, my head mess. Everywhere I turn mess, mess, mess. Mess and Bad Things are the recipe of my life.

Except now there's Mags. And she's no Bad Thing.

Somewhere, in the middle of all this stuff about breezes and storerooms and petrol and fireplaces and tins of powder and paraffin drums and rope and Hodge and Chuffer and Macker and Scotland and the Hand and the Cupboard and all their criss-crossing, was the right recipe explaining it all.

But what was it?

Mags reappeared. She was wearing trousers, polo neck, short denim jacket, scarf and pink bobble hat. Very frisky, Mags.

'Where's your coat?' she said.

'Left in a hurry this morning,' I said. 'Remember?'

Mags left the room and returned almost at once with a green parka.

Dodgy!

She saw my expression. 'It's a bit of history,' she said. 'My mum wore this on a thousand demos when she was a student. She won't mind.'

No – but I might, Mags. Nice one. I get to wear designer Oxfam in camouflage-green niffing of tear gas, baton-bruised and pressure-washed by water cannon.

Mags tossed it over.

A bundle of buttons clung to the lapels – Campaign

Against Cruelty to Cats, Animal Liberation, Save Our Planet, Stop Vivisection Now, League Against Cruel Sports, Stop Fox Hunting, Save the Fox – I was an anorak activist. Thanks, Mags. It was one badge missing: Ban Big Mothers!

'There's some woolly gloves in the pocket,' said Mags. 'It's going to be cold.'

I stared at her. Woolly gloves! Be serious, Miss Wilkinson. How much of a wozzeck do you think I am?

As it turned out, it was no night for wozzecks. But it was the night that Star came good.

17

A Big Burner

Mags wanted to get to The House early, before they lit the bonfire. I told her it was a two-storey job and nearly as high as the first floor where the snot slept, and that it would take all night to burn out. No hurry.

Jeff the caretaker had built it. Started in September, collecting stuff, stashing it out of Big Mother's way behind the boiler house. Last minute, he was going to put in a few old tyres to get the heat up and blow out some real spooky smoke. Jeff always took trouble. He wanted it bigger than the one at Glendale Comp. He hated Glendale, because he'd got fired from his job as caretaker there for nicking kitchen supplies, flour and sugar and stuff, and selling it on the sly. He said it was only charity work. 'Borrowing from the haves and handing to the haven'ts.'

Jeff was OK to us. To him, we were haven'ts Big Time. So, he was always good for a few freebies. 'Got any borrows, Jeff?' Borrows were fags and biscuits and things, never bought, just borrowed. 'You don't get much in this life,' he used to say. 'Just 'cos you borrow doesn't mean you're bent. We're all on borrowed time. So, I say, a bit more borrowing won't hurt.'

He used to say Big Mother was a borrower. Only she took from the haven'ts, that's us. 'Picking the pockets of the poor and defenceless,' he said.

That's a laugh. I thought of Hodge and Spaz. Defenceless, them? No way.

'She's screwing the Council. Creaming the lot of you,' he said.

'Creaming?' I said.

'Nicking. Fingering. Twocking. Stashing. Come on, Jez! You mean, you don't know? You little innocent. You little little innocent. She creams the clothing, and the maintenance. Stinges on the food. Stodges yer with porridge.'

And I remember thinking when I first heard all this, I should shop her. But who'd believe a haven't kid? No one. So we just got on with porridge and Tide-over mank.

This year the bonfire was special. It was Jeff's last. He was retiring and wanted to go out with a bang, with one last Big Burn.

I'm thinking as much about the fire as listening to Mags while we walk down the Donkey Path towards Lazarus House. She is mouthing on about Fat Fat Jane and something about a pair of leather trousers. 'The two just don't go. What she want to wear leather for?'

'All cows come in leather,' I say.

'Nasty one, Jez.'

'Suit you, Mags, would leather.'

She doesn't say anything, but her lips part in a shallow smile. It stays for a long time and then she starts to hum some tune or other.

Moments later, beyond the trees we can see a yellow glow, like as if some space ship has just landed and the after-burn of the engines is scorching the ground.

We push through the garden gate and emerge from under the trees into The House grounds. The bonfire is well away and Mags hurries forward. I'm more cautious. I hold back, searching through the crowds of kids standing round the inferno. No sign of Big Mother. No sign of her hulking around, just Jeff waving a long-handled rake, jabbing it at the flames, like he was poking at an angry bull to keep it at bay.

The fire-escape ladder is down and I notice a row of water buckets lining the path as we approach. Might put out a snot on fire, wouldn't touch Jeff's Big Burner.

Twenty metres away and we can feel the heat. I stop, still on the lookout, and notice a couple of the snot, each with a fist of rockets, big ones, standing nearby. I go over. Have a closer look.

They're *StarBusters* OK.

'Where you get those?' I say.

'Hi, Zippo. Thought you'd done a bunk. She's after you and she's keggin mad.'

'Yeah. Yeah. But where did you get these?'

'Your mate.'

'Hodge? He ain't my mate.'

'Not Hodge.'

It wasn't Hodge? I stop. Think. Who then? 'Not Macker?' I say.

'Yeah. Dead cheap, they were.'

'How many?' I say, beginning to realize I don't really want to know the answer.

'Loads.'

'Ten? Twenty?'

'Loads. He had them at that allotment place.'

I say nothing. They move off towards Jeff, who's in charge of the display.

I stare at the flames without seeing them. Mags is jumping up and down in front of me and clapping her hands. The flames unfurl and wave back.

Macker!!

What's going on? My good mate Macker, ripping me off? Going behind my back. No way. Macker wouldn't betray a mate. No way.

Then I remembered the trainers. I could see them again in my mind's eye. Keggin hell, Macker! Then I knew. They weren't Nike copy, five-quid repros. They were the real thing. MacNally had flogged all my stuff so he could get his sweaty feet into some serious-cost designer footwear.

I shook my head. It wasn't true, surely. Macker?

It was like waking up from an operation or something. The dark separates out, gets muzzy and muzzy, begins to get clearer.

Pictures. Pictures. Clear as daylight now. An old ladder. A length of rope. An empty mattress. The kitchen storeroom. Two abandoned *StarBusters*. The ash chute. The missing Macker.

I saw it in a flash, how it all fitted together. I had the recipe. Hodge didn't do Chuffer's hut. The storeroom wasn't Hodge's new hideaway. It was Macker's. That's why he'd never been around. He'd taken over the freaking storeroom so he could stuff himself from the kitchen and safely stash the fireworks he'd nicked.

I was vaguely aware of someone calling. Only when Mags grabbed my arm did I come to, my face flushed with the heat of the flames. They moaned and hissed at me. Deep orange, purply-red, their angry tails lashing and swishing the night air like a nest of dragons.

'What's up,' shouted Mags as Jeff sent up the first batch of *StarBusters*. They whooshed high, beyond the crinkly black branches of the trees, rose and rose, up, up into silence and then ... and then ... exploded and cast a thousand, thousand sparks which, like a net of silvered fish, fell back and drowned in the noiseless ocean of the night.

'Wicked,' said Mags. 'Come on, Jez. Something's up. Is it that Big Mother woman?'

I shook my head. 'It's about Macker.'

'Your mate, Macker?'

'My so-called mate.'

'Why? What's he done?'

I edged Mags away from the fire and towards the deep shade of a large tree. I explained about the *StarBusters* and the storeroom.

'But you said it was Hodge.'

'I know, but I was wrong.' I sighed. 'It's not like Macker, Mags. It's just not right. Macker wouldn't do this to me. I'm his mate.'

'Well, he's done it, whatever the reason.' Mags obviously wanted to get back to the fire. She began to wander away.

I held back.

It was a real Big Burner now, the flames mega and spitting sparks from their tips, which were feathering and black from the spent rubber and petrol.

Watching them, I began to feel, deep inside my mind, a little burn of my own kindling. Bit by bit, I could feel it growing. Brighter and brighter.

Then I remembered what Macker had said that time in the hut when we discovered the fireworks were missing. The exact words lit up in my head.

Remember, whatever happens, we're mates.

Whatever happens, Macker?

What had happened was, he'd trashed and stolen my fireworks, let me take the rap with Big Mother, lied to me and lost me a load of cred.

Bad Things, Big Time.

Was I supposed to lie down and take it like a mate?

Then more Macker words flashed and exploded inside me.

You have to do some bad things for the sake of one good thing.

A rocket whooshed in my head.

One good thing!

217

A huge flame reared and people staggered back from the thrust of its heat.

And I knew then what Macker was on about.

I shouted to Mags, who had stumbled back from the fire.

'Listen, it's about Macker. I think he's going to burn The House down. I think that's what all this is about.'

Mags snorted. 'Don't be such a wozzeck. That's bonkers.'

'No, not bonkers, Mags. Listen. Listen.' I held tight to her coat sleeve. I needed someone to listen first, and tell me I was bonkers after.

'I know it. He's going to torch The House. He talked about it, but I never thought he was serious. But Macker's changed. He was always a bit wobbly. Now he's really flipped. Something's switched in his head. Inside his brain, he's ticking away. He's like one of those suicide bombers – mad.'

'Doesn't mean he's going to do something stupid.'

'No, not something stupid, Mags, something so mega, it's going to light up the whole sky.'

Mags' face glowed orange from the brightness of the fire.

'Remember Chuffer's can of paraffin? His pink? And Maggot's can of petrol? I told you I found them in the storeroom. And the old clothes and that tin of gunpowder?'

I gripped Mags' arm tighter.

'I think Macker's going to stash all the polish and the oil drums together in a pile, then he's going to soak the old clothes in petrol and paraffin, and then he's going to stuff them underneath, and then he's going to climb out of the window, and then he's going to light a twist of rags and chuck them back through the window and *oompphh*. House on fire. It's the ideal place. The ceiling's wood . . .'

'And,' Mags interrupted, 'there's a good draught to get it going in no time. Oh my God!' she said. 'What are we going to do?'

We both looked at The House. It was lit at the front by the roaring fire, and somehow it looked flat, like a painting. All its dark dimensions seemed suddenly lost. All the Bad Things had flown away. It was like a giant-size doll's house.

Suddenly, we saw a familiar figure coming down the steps. Big Mother! She was wearing a cloak, and she held in her hand an electric torch whose light-beam danced before her.

I knew immediately that she'd be looking for me. One of the snots with the rockets had probably told her.

'Let's move,' I said to Mags.

We watched Big Mother turn at the bottom of the steps and begin shining the torch light into the bushes growing against The House, and into the dark recesses under trees and occasionally into their branches.

'Thinks I'm a monkey,' I said to Mags. We edged round so that the fire was between us and Big Mother.

Flames flush The House a rosy pink and their reflections glitter in the windowpanes. 'He's going to do it tonight,' I say to Mags again. 'I know it. Remember, he said he had something to sort out. This is it. Now's the time, when nobody's in the place.'

'Maybe we can stop him,' said Mags.

I looked at her. 'Stop him?' I said. 'I want it burnt to the ground.'

'But Macker might get killed or something. We can't just do nothing. You can't burn a building, just like that.'

Some things have to be burnt out, I was thinking. Burn out the Cupboard. Burn the rats and the wasping. Burn the duckings and the rattle of the Hand. Burn the beatings and the bruising. Burn Big Mother. Burn her. Burn her.

Suddenly, a light is blinding me and a hand closes painfully round my shoulder.

'Walker,' she hisses. 'Walker. Got you. And this time you're not going to get away.'

I scream.

'Stop it.' It is Mags shouting. 'Stop it. That's not fair.'

No rules here, Mags. Cosh time.

But what saved me wasn't Mags or the cosh, but the deep booming sound that seemed to echo from The House, not just in the air, but through the very ground we were standing on. It was only afterwards that we found out about the ancient tunnels, and realized that it was down their empty passages, running under our feet, that the runaway sound was escaping.

All the shrieks and the screams and the anguish of innocents were mixed up in that fury of noise. It deafened us and rumbled us, and then roared into echo, out and out, till it was swallowed into silence and the blankness of night.

Big Mother stood stock-still. Slowly the Hand uncurled and released its grip.

'What was that? What was that?' she said, almost panic in her voice.

Everyone was looking at The House. The bonfire crackled and roared on regardless.

'Oh my God,' said Mags slowly. 'Look.'

From some windows on the first floor, fire was spurting, and from the back of The House smoke was drifting over the roof, writhing and ghostly and faintly golden, bathed as it was by the bonfire's fierce burning.

'The House. The House. Fire. Fire,' shrieked Big Mother, stumbling forward.

'Round the back,' I shouted to Mags, and we dashed across the lawn.

18

Last of The House

There was no sign of Macker. The ground crunched underfoot. Glass. Glass everywhere. And the roar of flames and windows exploding. And smoke. And along the length of the storeroom window, a frill of yellow fire.

Did Macker get out?

Suddenly Mags was pulling at my arm. She said nothing, just pointed upwards.

From where we were, we had a good view of the top of the fire escape.

Standing there, waving its arms, was a dark figure.

'Macker,' I shouted. 'You keggin idiot!'

I turned to Mags. She was staring up, eyes wide open, just staring. 'He's going to jump,' she whispered hoarsely.

'Don't be daft.'

By now the flames had reached the second floor. An orange glow was rising and brightening all the rooms. Smoke-shadows loomed and lumbered through the dense light. I could see little red wings fly at the windows, like trapped birds frantic to escape.

Macker, Macker, get out . . . now!

Did he? Did he like.

No. He started dancing. Dancing in the inferno.

We watched him jigging up and down, like some little kid at a zoo seeing a monkey for the first time.

'He's mad,' said Mags. 'We've got to get him out.'

Mad all right, Mags. My mad mate, Macker. I half expected him to do a somersault and hang upside down from the railings.

I started to smile. Atta Macker. 'Go, gorilla,' I shouted. 'Go,' I roared. He raised both arms, roared back and began beating his chest. Mad Macker. Lord of monkeys. Kid Kong.

Mags was shouting something but I wasn't listening. I was laughing. Really laughing, sort of manic, like when you're on the top of a cliff and the wind is roaring hard and cold in your face and blowing the rest of the world away, so there's only you and the sky exploding in your ears. I roared and roared till my throat was burning with every breath.

Macker and me, mad boys again.

Then, gasping, I bent my knees, grinned my mouth wide and scratched at my armpits.

'Big Mother monkey,' I shouted, my voice ragged. 'Made a monkey of her. Bad monkey mother.'

Macker was laughing too, laughing and jigging and pointing at me with his curled gorilla finger.

It was old Macker time. Real monkey Macker. Real McCoy.

Atta Mac.

I reached up, curling my finger too.

Then he's calling, a small voice racing ahead of the fire growl. 'The Black Book. Gotta get the Black Book.'

'Let it burn, Macker. Just get out. Get down before it's too late, yer prat.'

Suddenly Mags was screaming in my face. 'What's it with you two? He's off his trolley. Can't you see? You both are. We've got to get him out, now, or it'll be too late.'

Before we could move, the dull moan of fire inside The House exploded into a roar above us as one of the windows shattered and glass showered down.

We ran to one side and looked up. The balcony was empty. Macker was gone.

'He's done it,' said Mags, horrified.

I ran to the bottom of the fire escape. No Macker. I leaned against the wall, breathing hard. Mags joined me.

'Is he?'

I shook my head.

'I'm going to get someone,' she said. 'Tell them.'

Just then a figure came charging round the corner. It was Jeff. 'You OK?' he said.

We nodded. 'But we need help,' said Mags. 'MacNally's still in there.'

'Christ!' said Jeff. 'Another prat. Fire engine's on its way. Hope they're in time.'

'Another prat?' said Mags.

'Yeah,' grunted Jeff. 'She's gone in as well. The fat lady.'

'Mrs Dawson? Big Mother?'

'That's the one. Get her stash, most likely. Get herself killed.'

Then I remembered Jeff's stuff about Big Mother selling us short, creaming off money for the kids for herself.

'A right scam,' said Jeff. 'Bleedin thousands off the Council.'

Freaking hell! Macker and Big Mother. Heading for the office, both of them. Macker for the book, Big Mother for the stash. She'd kill him.

'Come on,' Jeff was saying. 'You kids aren't safe here.'

Too late. I was seeing red and, inside of me, something was pounding to be out. I shook. I was rippling with anger, anger and fear, anger and fear. My fingers bent to claws, my neck stretched. I could see Macker and Big Mother locked together, swaying, reeling in and out of smoke, crashing through doors, she clawing at him, he ripping the book from her, spilling notes, tearing pages, thousands of them tumbling blindly into the roaring combustion.

I leapt at the escape ladder. 'He must have gone back in. I'm going to get him,' I shouted.

Mags made a grab for me. 'That's crazy,' she shouted. 'You'll get yourself killed. You'll both be killed.'

I stopped, my hands clamped to the metal ladder. 'I can't just leave him, Mags. Look, I'll go up here. I've done it before. I can do it in seconds. We can get out this way, no probs. Look, he's a mate, right.'

'And so am I,' she said. 'Aren't I? Why are you snarling at me? Why don't you listen to me? Why don't you do what I want?'

'Because you aren't stuck in a freaking fire.'

'OK. OK. But go, go. Now.'

Then she gave me a smack of a kiss and stepped back, her hand over her mouth, her eyes wide with shock. Kiss-shock, fire-shock? I didn't wait. I shinned up the escape like a regular monkey, bum fur aflame. I was on fire.

Near the top, I looked down to wave. Stupid or what! But, well, she'd kissed me, hadn't she?

No Mags left.

As I turned to climb through the window of Macker's room, a cloud of smoke fanned into the sky beyond the roof above me. I stared at it. Slowly it curled and stretched and flexed into a shape I knew well. 'Star,' I breathed. 'At last.'

Then he drifted – glided, more like – his dark fur tinged with orange, down the slope of the tiles and out of my view.

I was OK now. Star would look after me. Star would keep me safe. Star, and now Mags. No one could touch me now, not even Big Mother. She was history.

I clambered through the window.

No Macker.

I ran into the corridor, checked the lavs, checked the bogs. No Macker.

I dashed out, past my room and on to the top of the steps leading down to the second floor. Smoke, hazy and heavy with the stench of burnt paint, was gathering at the bottom of the flight. I leapt down two, three at a time. The landing was empty of all but smoke. The door to one dormitory was half open and I could see flames flapping like sheets around one of the beds.

He couldn't be in any of the other rooms, because from behind all the closed doors I could hear the fire growling and crackling. It was the snarl of a giant dog, red jaws at work gnawing timbers, splintering planking, slashing furniture. No one could live with such fury.

Star was at work.

From here you could look over the banister and down the stairwell to the basement, some four flights below. I leaned over and peered down. The whole of the ground floor was lost in thick, seething smoke which, as I watched, was rising slowly upwards.

I took off my coat, tied it round my waist, and listened. Nothing but the crunch of fire and great cracking sounds from below as if the cables and bands that held The House together were snapping one by one. Would it suddenly burst asunder and collapse in a heap of bones and ashes?

I had to find Macker.

I start down the next flight, then stop. Below me, on the next landing, I can see something. Something writhing, a strange animal in torment. The smoke thins for a moment, and I realize it's two figures clasped, arms roped round each other.

I watch as they stagger from the wall towards the top of the stairs, swaying and turning, veering first to one side, then the other, and only stopping when they smack into the banisters. For a moment they hang there, then they begin slowly spiralling and arcing downwards into the smoke, only the rail stopping them from toppling over and plunging into the welling below.

'Macker,' I shout.

But he can't hear me. She's got him in a bear hug. He's trying to free himself. I can see now she's got his arms pinned to his sides and she's squeezing the life out of him. I can see his shiny monkey head lolling.

'Macker, Macker,' I'm screaming as I race down the steps.

I plunge into the gasping smoke and hurl myself at the two of them, Macker and Big Mother. I can hear her grunt as I hit her, but it makes no difference. She's got him. She's going to crush him, burst his ribs. She's grunting like an animal. Macker is whimpering, last little gasps. I can see his eyes rolling and white.

Suddenly, behind, a door splinters, like it's been axed, and a wing of flame sprouts instantly, brightening the landing. I can see that they're at the head of the stairs. I hurl myself at the two of them again, pushing and shoving them. I kick at Big Mother's foot, nudge it over the first step. She starts to tumble. Macker goes too, on top as they crash downwards.

At the turn of the stairs, they stop. I leap down and drag Macker free. Big Mother lies still, her eyes closed and a faint gargling gathering in her throat. Her face is smudged with soot, patches of her hair are singed and burnt to stubble.

I pull Macker back up the stairs, out of the rising smoke. I drag him on to the landing, shouting at him to wake up. I slap his face, open his mouth, breathe into him hot, gasping air.

He stirs. I sit him up. Got to get to the fire escape before the whole place goes up. On the top landing, as I look up, I can see flames fingering through the open banisters. Macker begins to stir. I get my hands under his armpits and hoist him upright. 'Walk,' I shout.

He starts to sort of walk. I get his arm round my shoulder, mine round his back and half-haul, half-push him upwards.

'That you, Jez?' I hear him mutter. 'You're a mate.'

'You're a monkey,' I say. 'Gorilla weight. Try walking.'

We're nearly at the top of the flight. I'm pushing him now, because he's getting steadier on his feet and is helping by pulling himself up on the banister rail.

All we've got to do is get up the stairs to my corridor, and then we can make the fire escape and we're out.

I can feel the smoke thick in my mouth now and sudden gusts of warm air pressing over us. I feel exhausted. I take a rest. Just a second, that's all I need. Macker is moving on his own. He's ahead. He's going to be OK. The Monkey Boys are nearly safe. It's a breeze now.

We're at the top of the stairs again. On our way up and out.

Macker's disappeared. The smoke's got him, but he'll be OK. He's got to be now.

I'm coughing and kneeling down. Just taking a breath. No worries. Not far. Almost there.

Then –

Something closes over my ankle. Clamps tight.

I'm slipping backwards.

I twist round, grab a rail, look down.

Big Mother!

I don't know whether she's pulling me down or pulling herself up.

I hold the rail tight. Monkey-grip it.

229

She's wheezing hard. And her eyes are wide open, and I can see the pupils, black but empty, like the ends of two gun-barrels staring straight at me. Her face is white, chalk-white, death-white, dead dog-white, like the dead dog I once saw in the canal. All this flashes across my mind.

Her mouth opens and her teeth chatter as if she's biting at the air.

I try and wrench my foot free. I squeal in pain. Then I realize she's got me in the Hand.

'Star,' I scream. 'Star. Quick.'

I can see her nostrils and her lips. They're sooted up, like she's been breathing out smoke, like she's been eating it, breathing it, eating it.

Big Mother's going to eat me.

She's pulling me down, tugging and tugging. She's slipping down the stairs and I'm going with her, my whole body stretching. I can feel my grip on the railing slip.

'Star. Help. Star.'

I kick out with my free leg.

I'm slipping further. I bring my heel down on the Hand. I kick at it. Kick at it. Kick at it.

She's so strong, so strong.

'Star.' My voice is hoarse.

No reply.

Then, suddenly, on a landing above, there's a crash, like a window shattering, and a door blows open. Thick clouds of smoke roll out.

I jerk at the sound and swing my trapped leg hard against a rail. The hold slackens. I wrench my foot free.

I'm on my back and pushing upwards, away from Big Mother's flailing fingers.

She's on her knees and is scrambling after me.

She is so big, so fast.

I get to the landing, still kicking. But she's on me, on my legs the whole weight of her. I manage to curl my body round the banister post so my cheek rests on the floor. My arms are wrapped round an upright, and only my legs are hanging down the stairs.

Oh God!

She's crawling up and over me. She's going to smother me. Smother me. I struggle to topple her off. I squirm. I shove. She loses her balance a bit, but she still has me. Now she starts jabbing at my face with the Hand, jabbing through the railings, ramming and ramming it at me, the claw fingers groping for my eyes. Her mouth is dribbling.

I'm going to die.

'Mags! Star. Help me.'

It's mouse squeak. Nothing more.

Suddenly I feel her weight lighten. I squirm half free. She throws her arm across my thighs to hold me down. She's shaking, like she's having a fit.

Then I see what's happening. She's pulling at the wooden Hand, wrenching at it, and I realize it's trapped between the rails. The thing is trapped, and she can't get it out. I'm breathing heavily, and I'm grinning too. And laughing. Great big monkey laughs. The Hand is caught. Big Mother's trapped. She's going to die.

Star's got the Hand in his jaws. He won't let go. No way.

Then she goes still. I go still.

I can hear monkey laughter everywhere. It's inside the rooms, in the chatter of fire behind the doors. It's in the whistle and hiss of the wood. In the wheeze and gasp of every dying flame.

Neither of us is moving.

Is she dead?

Through the railings I see curtains from below, ragged with fire, rise in the up-draught, the flames climbing up themselves, swirling their red tails as they pass us, cackling, towards the high ceiling above.

Suddenly her body shudders. The shake runs through me. The soft weight of her, the blubber of her is still trying to squash me, suck me into her, swallow me.

She is dead.

I feel vomit rising. I kick and I wriggle and I squirm free and clamber out of reach.

I'm standing at the top of the stairs, full of hard breathing, looking down on her. A deep growling rises up from the stairwell. It's Star's. He's coming. He'll have her. Tear the witch apart.

I turn. I'm free now.

'Help me.'

I look back.

She's staring at me. But the eyes are empty. 'Help,' she mouths, her good hand slowly flailing at the air, the fingers pleading.

*

Something crashes and thuds below. A spout of sparks glitters in the rising smoke and dies. Suddenly I feel Star, beside me. I can feel his hot breath. On my back.

'Help,' she whimpers.

'Star?'

He nods.

I take a step down. I roll up her sleeve. The Hand is bound to a stump of the forearm by leather straps. I fumble with the buckles, my eyes blurred by the smoke, now denser than ever.

She's quietly moaning.

I tear at the leather and yank the wooden thing away. As the claws snap together, one of them rips at my arm. I smash it down on the banister. The fingers curl up. Then I hold it aloft. It's like I've ripped the heart out of some monster. Blood trickles down my wrist. I'm coughing smoke.

Then I hurl it into the flames below. It plunges into the hot crunch of waiting jaws.

I look down at Big Mother. She blurs. I shake away the giddiness. My head swims a little, even so.

It's not her. Not her at all.

It's an old woman lying on the stairs, grey hair crinkling in the heat, bloodless face smeared in soot.

Just an old woman.

*

That's all.

Almost.

Someone has me by the coat collar. It's Star. I can tell. I can feel the hum of his breathing. The long hiss, the slow gasp of his effort. His big, soft mouth has me. He's pulling me towards the window, out of the smoke into air. I can feel his growl tremble in me.

Then –

It was all white. Then it was all black again. Then it was white. Then the colour came. I remember red. Especially red. 'Cos that was the colour of Mags' lips as she bent over me in the hospital.

Evidently my first words were: 'Macker?'

Later, when the effect of smoke eating had worn off a bit, and I could sit up in bed, she said she didn't really mind – about saying Macker was my mate, my special mate. It was obvious, she said, that I was in shock. I probably didn't know what I was saying. I was so high on drugs and stuff, I probably thought she was the pink rabbit.

No, Mags. There's only one rabbit here, and that's me. I've been down the hole most of my life. But now I'm out. Dream's over. It's wake-up time.

I slump back on the pillow, exhausted.

Then Mags says: 'But it was me told them where to find you. The firemen.' She nodded and smiled.

I grinned and squeezed her hand. 'Thanks, Mags.' What else can you say when someone's saved your life? Maybe I should get her some of that mystique stuff.

I thought back to Macker.

'So what happened to him?' I asked. 'Where is he? When's he coming to see me? Has he been? How long have I been out?'

'I think you should lie down,' said Mags. 'You don't look at all well.'

I stared at her. I suddenly felt my back go cold.

'Mags?' I grabbed her arm. 'Mags, what's happened?'

She didn't say a word. She didn't have to. She was looking at the floor.

Oh my God, Macker!

I thought back to the fire. It was all so fuzzy. The memories drifted past. I made a grab for one.

I was at the top of some stairs. Macker was ahead of me. The smoke came down. He disappeared.

'But he only had to find his way along the corridor outside my room, Mags, find his door, get through the window and down the fire escape. He could easily have got out. Easily.'

'They never found him,' said Mags. 'I'm sorry, Jez. So sorry.' She had her hands together, like you do when you have to pray, and they were over her mouth and tears had begun.

I swallowed hard and it hurt in my throat. Neither of us said anything.

Not for ages.

Then Mags opened up, her voice wobbling. 'He could have just vanished in the smoke and the confusion. He's probably in Scotland by now, like he said.'

I stared across the ward. 'Probably,' I echoed. 'Probably. Scotland, Macker's vanishing point.'

Through the window, I could see a white cloud floating in a watery blue.

'He must be,' sniffed Mags. 'If there's no sign, he must have got away, mustn't he? Must have.'

I nodded.

The House was an ash pit. It was like a cremation, I thought. Where are you, among so much ash?

In my mind's eye, I turned away from the smouldering ruin of The House and, instead, looked back over the big trees in the garden, beyond the allotments and Chuffer's hut, beyond Appleton and the canal, and all the way up England, over the hills to Scotland. Where my mate Macker was all alive and grinning.

I'm watching him now, hanging by one arm from the Celtic crossbar, after the match was well over. Gorilla goalie, star of the team, my mate Macker.

'He's back in the jungle,' I said. 'Where he belongs.'

Mags smiled. She liked the idea of Macker swinging through the trees.

She laughed through her tears. I began to laugh too. Monkey laughter. And we went on laughing well into eating the cake her mum had baked for me. It hurt, laughing and swallowing, but what did it matter! In my head, Macker was right there.

As she was leaving, Mags said: 'And they didn't find Big Mother either. After they got you out, they went back for her, but she was gone.'

Gone!

No way. Big Mother's there all the time, where the Bad Things are. She's the mank inside us all.

And she's inside me now, smoke pouring out of her mouth, fuzzing my head.

Curse the witch.

'I'll be back later,' she said.

As I drifted off I realized it was Mags talking to me.

Yeah, come back, Mags, soon. I can't fight her on my own.

Next thing, I was being gently shaken awake. It was the nurse with Dave. My social worker. I closed my eyes. 'Can you hear me, Jez?' he said very quietly.

'Only if you speak up, Dave.'

'You OK?'

Sure, Dave. Top of the world. Except some witch just tried to strangle me, then eat me. I've been torched alive. I'm the barbecue boy, the original kebab kid. I've been coshed out for hours, days, I dunno. My lungs feel like old wrapping paper. I can hardly breathe. My throat's like I've swallowed hot needles.

OK?

Sure, Dave. Just an average ten minutes in your average hand-me-down kid's life.

'Good news, Jez. I've got you a placement. Very supportive environment.'

Environment! Stuff you, Dave. What do you think I am? A laboratory rat? It's not a cage I want. It's a home. A home, Dave.

I opened my eyes.

'It's the least we can do in the circumstances,' he was saying.

Knowing you, Dave, it *would* be the least you could

do. Thanks, but no thanks. You can stuff your circumstances. I want my own circumstances. And just at
the moment I've got all the circumstances I need. Nice
people. Clean sheets. No rats. No scams. No pee. No
floor polish. No Hodge.

'Well, Jez? Have you nothing to say?'

Nothing.

Dave yacked on. 'We are on your side, you know? I
wouldn't want you to think you're on your own. We
take our duty of care to protect children like yourself
very seriously. Very seriously indeed. OK?'

I could hear his voice getting distant like he was on the
other side of a wall in a different room.

You thought Big Mother was OK, Dave. And all the
time she was leading you by the nose, you prat. Creaming
you like all the others. At The House the only protection on offer was the sort we paid Hodge fags for. Where
were you when she wasped Macker? Where were you
when she locked me in the Cupboard? Where were
you when she smashed me with the Hand?

Then Dave came right out with it. 'You're going to
Ramage Hall. It's a new residential school. Floodlit
five-a-side, state-of-the-art computer suites, telly in every
room. You'll love it. Not many kids like you get a chance
like this.'

'Where the hell's Ramage Hall?'

'I had to really push for this one, Jez. It's a great place.
Believe me, you'll just love it.'

'Where the jig is it, Dave?' I struggled to sit up.

'I hope you appreciate what we're doing here. It's for
your own good.'

I lay back on the pillow, pretending to doze.

For my own good, Dave? Don't make me laugh.

Through my half-opened eyes I could see him sitting there, scribbling in a notebook.

Then I heard someone whispering in my ear.

It was Star.

Star was back, smoke still clinging to his fur.

He told me to listen carefully.

Dave, he said, was up to something.

That's no surprise, I said. Soon as they say it's for your own good you know they want to shut you up, put four walls round you and forget the key.

Ramage Hall? Sounded like some heap in the country. Why are they sending me miles away, Star?

Trying to smooch you with computers and floodlit footie, he said.

But why couldn't they get me a foster in Appleton? I could still see Mags, go to my old school, laugh at Dimmo, give Fat Fat the finger, sort out Maggot, chew tea with old Chuffer.

Because Dave's scared of you, said Star. He wants you out of the way.

Scared of me? Out of the way? Why?

Remember the inspectors, the 'interferers', as Big Mother called them?

I nodded.

Think about it, said Star.

I did.

And then, bit by bit, I began to see what he was getting at.

After the fire there'd be even more inspectors. They'd

239

have an enquiry. All the Bad Things would come out. They'd ask questions.

'Dave,' I said, 'these inspectors, they'll be asking questions, right?'

He nodded slowly and looked at me, suspicious like.

'What sort of questions, Dave?'

He shrugged. 'About The House, I suppose. What happened there.'

'You mean about wasping, Dave, and bullying, Dave, and the Hand, Dave, and the Cupboard, Dave?'

Silence.

'What do I say when they ask me about you, Dave?'

'How do you mean, about me?'

'Well, about you and the wasping and the smacking and the ratting and stuff.'

'I didn't know anything about those things.'

'Everyone else knew. Mrs Wilkinson knew. Miss Chips at school knew. Jeff the caretaker knew. Thirty kids knew. Looks like you were the only one who hadn't a clue what was going on, Dave. Pity, that, because you were the one supposed to protect us. Weren't you?'

Good one, said Star.

I waited a bit.

'I'll just say you didn't know what was going on, shall I?'

He stared at me.

'Or shall I say you turned a blind eye? Or shall I say you did all you could to protect us vulnerable kids because you had a duty of care which you took so seriously you never lifted a single finger to stop the Bad Things?'

'You little shit,' he said, teeth clenched.

Watch it, Dave. I know your game. You want me out of the way so I won't blow the gaff, as my friend Chuffer would say, so I can't dump the dirt on you.

Well, forget it, Dave. I'm not one of your dimmo kids any more who always does what Daddy D says.

That's right, sock it to him, said Star.

Then I looked Dave straight in the eye. Like Star told me.

'You see, Dave. I don't really fancy this Ramage place. I don't think it's appropriate in the circumstances, do you? Not the right environment!'

He nodded slowly. 'Not the right environment,' he repeated like a zombie.

Then Star nudged me.

Remember, Mags said you could stay at her place, he whispered.

I smiled.

'OK, Dave? Glad you agree. No Ramage. Now I know a better place I can go for a bit. A real home. Where I get cared for. You'd want that, wouldn't you?' I paused. 'Well, how about it?'

He turned and stared at me. He looked like he'd seen the ghost of Big Mother standing in front of him. He was that pale.

'You won't tell them, will you?' he whispered at last. 'You don't mean it, do you? You can't. I'll lose my job.'

'You'll lose more than your crappy job, Dave. You'll go to prison.'

Let him sweat on that, said Star. Let him think it over.

Eventually I said: 'You've got to fix it so I can stay with these friends of mine.'

He looked puzzled. 'What friends?'

'The Wilkinsons.'

'You've got to be joking.'

'No.'

'But they're the ones complained about The House. Busybodies. Ignorant do-gooders. No male role-model there. Pushy girl. Not your sort.'

Prat! What do you know about my sort, Dim D, mega do-no-gooder?

He was shaking his head.

Right, Dave. We'll play it your way.

'Get me the phone,' I said. 'I want the police.'

'OK, OK,' he said, looking round anxiously in case someone had heard me. 'I'll do it. I'll do it. No need to shout. I'll sort it with the Wilkinsons. Just a short-term measure.' Then he paused, looked round again to see if anyone was near enough to hear, leaned forward and said. 'But you've got to promise. Say nothing. Right? To the inspectors?'

I closed my eyes.

'Promise. Promise.'

'Sort me out,' I said, putting a right croak in my voice. 'And I'll think about it.'

At this point the nurse came over.

'You mustn't tire him,' she said.

I opened my eyes just enough to see.

242

She helped Dave get up, he was that bricked.

'You all right?' she said. 'You look as though you've seen a ghost.'

I sank back into the pillow. I was wrecked.

Thanks, Star.

'Pushy', eh!

He called Mags pushy. Well, I don't mind that, Dave, a girl being pushy about me. In fact, it makes me feel good all the way through. Because, out there, in the world of beatings and wasping and bullies and whips and ratting and placements and protection rackets, where all the Bad Things are, someone is pushing for me.

Just me.

Someone who doesn't think I'm a caseload of mank, a number, a tick-in-a-box, a no-no, a yob on a stick to be licked into shape.

Thanks, Mags. See ya soon. After the smoke blows away.

But the smoke doesn't blow away. Not just yet.

Instead, it thickens inside my head, gathering like dark clouds, and soon they are sweeping over me and it's tempest dark, then grope-black.

Next, I'm swinging in a hammock. And it's a dream. And it's true. It's a summer's day. It's Mags' garden. I am spattered with sunlight. And above me the tree is full of pink rabbits. All singing.

It was only later, when all the lights were out, that the Black Witch, Big Mother, came back and woke me up.

243

Tap. Tap. Tap.

I knew she was at the bottom of the bed. I could hear her wheeze. I could feel her hand pressing on the blanket, fingers out for me.

I sat up, my forehead damp, my heart twanging.

I tried to shout help, but mouse-squeak was all I'd got. It was the smoke eating. It just does your voice in.

But there was no one there. She was dust and ash, like Macker. Like us all.

I stared across the room and through the window and out into the night.

The stars were sprinkled in billions and trillions. I began looking, scanning heaven's oceans for him, like I used to in The House. 'Where are you, Star? Where are you?'

No answer.

I could wait. I knew Star. He could be gone for days. He has a life of his own. At this very moment, he'll be racing through the interstellar meadows, scattering the star-chaff hither and thither in his wake. I love it, the way he tosses his head from side to side, and I love it when the silver seeds stick to his dark, shining coat. And I love the way he nuzzles through whole constellations, his snout dusted with the breath of their light.

I love you, Star. Goodnight, Star.